E Z R A ' S   G H O S T S

EZRA'S

STORIES

GHOSTS

Darcy Tamayose

NeWest Press

NeWest Press wishes to acknowledge that the land on which we operate is Treaty 6 territory and a traditional meeting ground and home for many Indigenous Peoples, including Cree, Saulteaux, Niitsitapi (Blackfoot), Métis, and Nakota Sioux.

Library and Archives Canada Cataloguing in Publication
Title: Ezra's ghosts : stories / Darcy Tamayose.
Names: Tamayose, Darcy, author.
Identifiers: Canadiana (print) 20210207221 | Canadiana (ebook) 20210207272 | ISBN 9781774390474 (softcover) | ISBN 9781774390481 (ebook)
Classification: LCC PS8639.A554 E97 2022 | DDC C813/.6—DC23

Editor for the Press: Leslie Vermeer
Cover and interior design: Natalie Olsen
Cover photo: Matt Lief Anderson/Stocksy.com
Author photo: Taylor Novakowski
Excerpt from "Nōhkom, Medicine Bear" by Louise Bernice Halfe used by permission.

 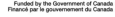

NeWest Press acknowledges the support of the Canada Council for the Arts, the Alberta Foundation for the Arts, and the Edmonton Arts Council for support of our publishing program. We acknowledge the financial support of the Government of Canada through the Canada Book Fund for our publishing activities.

#201, 8540-109 Street
Edmonton, Alberta T6G 1E6
NeWest Press   www.newestpress.com

No bison were harmed in the making of this book.
Printed and bound in Canada   22 23 24 25   4 3 2 1

for Taylor and CJ

CONTENTS

The Thesis

1

Ghostfly

25

The Ryukyuan

123

Redux

239

THE

THESIS

November 28, 2019 —

WHERE DO I BEGIN?
In the middle. I'll start in the middle.
And then I'll scribble my way to the end.

Comments on the right-hand margin of my thesis indicate that my supervisor has seen a novelistic tendency in my academic writing. Academic imposter. I don't claim to know for sure, but suspect. There's some resistance. When cognitively wiped out or bored, I default to pencil and marginalia. Dubious, in a subaltern way, of those timeless theorists who possess almost cultish intellectual legacies. Constricted by the spheres of complex methodologies that seem overdue for a cultural overhaul. These books, the study, discourse, exploration, epistemology, heuristics — in crafting their complex academic identities surely the journey began with pencil in hand.

Samuelsson, Edward
November 11, 2019
This recent habit of novelization seems to distract from the formal aspect of your thesis, Nick. For the sake of academic authority you ought to refrain. Do recognize the pre-established boundaries of creative and academic. Maintain the rigorous analysis. Keep within your proposed framework.

One of my first jobs as freelance illustrator was for a home furnishings company with a retro-aesthetic communications strategy. In fact, most of my paltry income back then came from this work.

Furniture Illustrator Process
1) Take reference photos both Polaroid and digital of the furniture to be illustrated
2) Pencil sketch
3) Wood grain and detailing using Rapidograph pen*
4) Erase any sign of graphite without smudging

Addiction ... slow drag of the line.

This was a time in my life when I began to cultivate patience and more evident idiosyncratic tendencies. I could draw for hours at a time. Sometimes even long into the night, until my body became stiff. And I would often have to shake out my hands as the fingers would cramp. Like chess, there were many ink moves of different kinds. To the left, right, diagonally, crosshatch, stipple, and such. I'm certain my hand developed its own cybernetics and means of predicting outcomes. And when I had a mental breakdown many years later as a still-struggling artist, that right hand had gained so much experience wielding the 2H,

---

* The Koh-I-Noor Rapidograph pen was often used by draftsmen and illustrators. The consistent ink flow produced a clean line.

5B, tech pen, felt pen, conté, and sumo brush that it became my autopilot. Soon, in order to pay my bills, I diversified and began to write copy. It took quite some time, but I taught myself to write in the same manner of discipline as with illustrating.

I've taken up sketching less these last years while in post-secondary studies and writing more — not copy, but essays. Yet I always miss those long stretches devoted to drawing. Is it a crutch, then, in theory, that I have integrated this creative literary style into my thesis? Have I combined the feeling that drawing gives with formal academics, resulting in, as Samuelsson says, a kind of novelization of my thesis? Maybe just call it an inclusive transdisciplinary path. But likely it's a manifested hybrid output as the result of a long-ing for creative practice — one that the formality of a thesis doesn't quite deliver (for me).

What if some things are so personal that they are un-attainable?

Arguably (and that matters in academic writing, it seems), formal critical analysis of art or discourse deconstructs the very mystical and unspeakable qualities that it stands on. Is this something Barthes was alluding to? I'm not quite sure as I've only just begun to listen to podcasts about Barthes. When I was young and the library held all the answers, I read something that I've always come to connect to Henry Moore the sculptor. I can never quite remember verbatim.

Though that may be intentional. The quote, if I remember correctly, is related to the tradition of analyzing textuality, and then attempting to use the same theoretics to analyze and demystify art.* Yes, I think so.

Anyways, back to the necessary logic of the world: it seems my supervisory committee has a proposition they'd like to discuss. Meeting tomorrow. There's no need for me to be worried.

---

* "It is a mistake for a sculptor or a painter to speak or write very often about his job. It releases tension needed for his work. By trying to express his aims with rounded-off logical exactness, he can easily become a theorist whose actual work is only a caged-in exposition of conceptions evolved in terms of logic and words." Henry Moore (1937). See Philip James, *Henry Moore on Sculpture: A Collection of the Sculptors Writings and Spoken Words* (London: Macdonald, 1966).

January 6, 2020 —

Just landed. Still on plane.

how was trip?

Sat by cougher. Whole trip.

annoying

Talk later. We're all moving.

okay ♥

Nick Holt
To: Kate MacNeale
Re: libraries

Hi Kate,

How are you? Any morning sickness?

Lying in bed.

Just finished reading a bit from New York Times. Chinese edition. Every morning slipped under the door. Pages and pages. Logographics.

So grateful to the committee for funding this trip. Ryukyuan research. Not the same without you, though.

Today was at the National Library of China. Thread-bounds, sutras, maps. A kingdom of resources. Sketching madly.

Remember Cambridge last summer? Plenaries. Tolkien. Artificial intelligence. International development. Haunted Selwyn Library. You. Me. That. And making love in Ann's Court with the windows wide open to the cool breeze, crescent moon, and sifting of stardust.

Miss you,

Nick

Nick Holt January 11, 2020 at 11:51 PM
To: Kate MacNeale
Re: great wall

Hi Kate,

Any cravings? Let me guess. Old Dutch potato chips. Plain.

Great Wall. Grand. Old. Crumbly. Hard to believe humans built it.
Walked. Sketched. I wonder, how would Sima Qian write history
if he were alive today?

Remember the research we did on the Shang dynasty? Oracle bones. Tortoise shells. That one sentence in the essay ... haha. Instead of "be divined" you wrote "bee divined." Samuelsson missed it, gave you an A+. We laughed so hard. One of those moments when nerds lose it.

Katherine ...

bee divined,

Nick

April 11, 2020 —

Home.

I finally found my way home.

But she ignored me.

Upset that I had gone to China without her, I suspect. I don't know for sure. She hasn't spoken to me.

The spring sunlight rimmed her hair as she came in from the screen door in the back. Her hair was lit. Bangs covering her brows, eyes cast down, and long lashes fanned. I am reminded of the time she walked the shore that one morning in Okinawa, 2014. Summer studies at the University of the Ryukyus. She had always looked so beautiful without makeup. Those freckles and crooked ears.

Unusually warm outside at this time. Multitudes of tulips.

She walked up the three steps and into the kitchen, passed me as if I weren't there. She had been so distant lately. Depressed, it seems. She pulled off the garden gloves, washed her hands. Bright-coloured tulips in a tall glass vase.

Coffee still warm. I watched her pour from that large hourglass flask. She had turned the coffee-making process

11

into something of an art and a ritual with the scale, grinder, and cast-iron kettle. Kosemura played on Spotify. Crisp piano runs prowled the walls and ceilings — and in one uninterrupted sentence filled the kitchen corners then the seams then the spaces between the floor boards then coalesced with the morning light. She sat across from me. Held her favourite mug and looked out the window.

"I like the sky today. Do you?" I think she acknowledged this.

A robin landed on the sill. Kate continued to gaze out the window to the sky.

"The trip was essential — for my master's research. I needed to study the navigational markers."

Once again, she seemed to nod. So I went on.

"For Imperial China, Diaoyu* was a stop on the way to the Ryukyuan Kingdom. I couldn't pass up the grant to work in China, Kate." Tears fell. I had heard that pregnancy brings about unpredictable emotions. Yet . . . those tears and the tenderness seemed to terrify me for some reason.

---

* This resource-rich remote island group situated in the East China Sea is under territorial dispute. Nomenclature based on perspective: Diaoyu (China), Tiaoyutai (Taiwan), and Senkaku (Japan). In ancient times the emperor of China would send ships to the Ryukyuan Kingdom. Along the way they would stop at these islands.

Nick Holt
To: Kate MacNeale
Re: night

Hi Kate,

How are you? How's everything in Ezra? The Weather Network says a snowstorm there.

I've texted Otto to help with shovelling that driveway before too long. Best to get on that before the drifts become unmanageable. Otherwise we'll be snowbound like last winter. He's got a blower and a plow — he can figure it out. Don't shovel in your condition, 'kay?

Samuelsson's colleague is here from the University of the Ryukyus doing research on the islands. I'm going to be travelling alongside him. Dr. Iwao Miyagi. Teaches international law. It seems one of his research foci has to do with the territorial dispute of the islands.

So today, we left Beijing to study the archipelago. The five islands. We went by boat. Similar to the one you and I took from Okinawa to Hamahiga Island. But these islands are in between the southern Ryukyus and Taiwan.

I can see why these small islands may have been a stopover for seafarers in ancient days. Stepping stones.

The sea was a little wild, as Bashō might suggest.

Maybe that's why I feel like shit. Seasick.

Love you lots,

Nick

April 19, 2020 —

Sun unusually bright.

She was sitting on the floor in a corner of the living room, surrounded by books.

Of course she was.

I watched her from across the room. She had her camera out.

Of course she did.

The natural light was full of promise. She was wearing her cotton shirt that was the colour of pale mint. It went well with her red hair. That green of fresh air. You know, to achieve that colour you have to be really careful about the amount of green you mix into white. You have to go almost one drop at a time. Her glorious mane was tied back. A few long tendrils fell gently and framed her exquisite face. It was true there was a glow. She was thumbing through books and papers in search of something specific. She hadn't seen nor heard me. I carried on into the kitchen.

The glass coffee flask on the counter, cone filter already in the mouth, beans brimming in the grinder. She had the blinds, doors, windows open — the other unusual thing about this early morn was that it was already hot. Not a huge surprise as residents are familiar with extreme weather.

Kate always loved her flowers. There were vases everywhere in the house, it seemed. Every kind and every colour. Except there were no lilies. She was allergic to them.

Suddenly the wind picked up. The sky was brilliant pink, the clouds seemed about to burst. "Kate!" I shouted, rushing into the living room. I wanted to let her know that the sky would be perfect for photos right now. She wasn't there. I glimpsed the papers stacked on the books. It was her Imperial China essay that she wrote for Samuelsson's course — the one she got an A+ on:

Writing can be rooted in China as early as 1200 BCE

when the Shang dynasty inscribed messages to

their god, di, on ox scapula and turtle plastron.

The bones would be put to heat and the cracks

that appeared would bee divined.

Nick Holt
To: Kate MacNeale
Re: late at night

Dear Kate,

It's your morning. My evening.

Hmm . . . nine thirty a.m. for you. So you've likely been up for a couple hours already. Coffee in hand. Maybe a slice of that raisin cinnamon bread from the Hutterite colony. Maybe cheese toast. You've got a playlist going. Let me guess. Something atmospheric and haunting. Maybe.

Ha! Okay.

I texted Otto yesterday. Seems his snow-clearing services are in demand this week. Cars high-ended in the middle of even Main Street, and beneath it all is black ice. Wind chill minus 40? A chinook in sight? Please be careful out there.

How much have you heard about this coronavirus?

Over here it's a huge deal. They are even planning to lock down a city called Wuhan. It's got a population of 11 million people! This is going to sound like paranoia, but when the weather clears, pick up a few of these items: surgical masks, toilet paper, and antibacterial hand sanitizer.

Love,

Nick

April 22, 2020 —

Out for an early-morning walk.

The back lane rolls out before us.

No one in sight either behind or ahead. I simply followed quietly with hands clasped behind my lower back. I was testing out which way was best to walk. I decided it was not as comfortable as letting my hands swing to my sides.

It was provincially week two of self-isolating and social distancing. In as much as Ezra normally demonstrated panic, you could say it had set in. Schools and institutions were quickly closing, all but essential businesses shutting doors. Grocery stores struggled to keep the shelves stocked with items such as toilet paper and hand sanitizer. The unthinkable was happening. Travel restrictions imposed and citizens urged to go home. Reluctance to take in passenger ships or refugee vessels. First, cities were in lockdown. Then countries closed. Mortality rates climbed. It was an Olympic event no country wanted to win. In the news: China, then Italy, and then, as the world watched in horror, the United States could not control the virus.

THE CITY OF EZRA was quiet as we walked.

I thought I could smell lilacs. But too soon for the blooms.

Perhaps it was Kate.

The sound of chimes in the distance from one of the houses. Not sure which one.

The quiet came forward in flickerings like that. Birds responded to wind chimes, faint florals pressed upon passing, a leaf travelled alongside a fence. Things that I didn't even know mingled, fraternized with one another. Had they been doing so all along?

How many worlds are we unaware of?

Right before us. Around us. Within us. How many?

Someone had left a broken wicker chair and a three-legged coffee table in the lane with hopes that, despite the pandemic arrest, City services like the annual Spring Clean-up would still take place. The broken wicker clattered gently in the breeze.

She had gone ahead. Exceptionally hurried today.

I ran to catch up. "Wait."

Nick Holt January 17, 2020 at 7:23 AM
To: Kate MacNeale
Re: about light

Dear Kate,

I'm in a Beijing hospital. But don't worry. It's just a precaution.

They've been tracking down all the passengers from the flight. A bit of a delayed post-quarantine. And since we spent so much time together with the trip to the islands, Miyagi — guilty by association — is here, too.

You'd love the natural light that fills this room in the mornings. A presence. There is a large leafy maple tree between the room and the sun. The leaves are diaphanous, you know, and when the tree moves with the wind, the sunlight and sun-shadows brush about the walls. My words are inadequate. This light.

But I'm tired now.

Love,

Nick

April 25, 2020 —

She was several steps ahead of me.

Her cell phone rang.

"Yes, Mom. Thank you."

She got into the car. She hadn't been driving much these days. No one had been.

"Where are we going?" I asked, crawling into the passenger side.

She had her *Pretty in Pink* playlist going.

Excellent posture. Kate always did have sensible posture. It was natural.

We drove. I watched her drive. She had the window halfway down. Her red hair was blowing back. Her eyes sparkled — deep green emeralds in the early morning. The light washed memory over her, then onto the steering wheel, then over the dash. I followed the memory around the car to the back seat. Flowers and books. She always had a book or two back there for whenever she drove to Henninger Lake to read. In the back seat now were a few books, including a resource textbook, Hein and Selden's *Islands of Discontent*. Not exactly a light read.

It wasn't until we went over the familiar shake of the old mill tracks that separated the northside of Ezra from the southside that I became more lucid. At least that was my self-perception (which is always somewhat suspicious). I had been feeling weak and feverish lately. Semi-repressed, in and out of clarity — not quite myself.

Meanwhile, she had cut right through the city, the Garfield Hockey Arena, Overpass #3, Overpass #2, Overpass #1, Dover Road where all the heritage houses tried to outshine one another, then the contrast of derelict and abandoned buildings in Stanton leading to Scenic Drive. Despite my preoccupation with Kate, I gazed out to the endless open sea of coulee horizon.

This road was my favourite stretch, with heaving coulees that rolled over the Ezra prairie. On this morning the landscape felt like me. A strange kind of confluence. I held my hand up to the sky. Astonished. The sun shone through my hand as through vellum. I had drawn on vellum once in a former life. The ink from a technical pen flows best on vellum, producing pure liquid filaments with no obstruction — no debris from random paper fibres. I moved my fingers as if drawing in the air. The sun exposed every tiny bone in my hand and its complex venous parish. Oddly, the unison was binarily glorious and furious.

Kate passed the small chapel on the hill where, on this morning, the tall stained-glass windows met the bright sun with astonishing beauty. Then she took the turnout into Ezra Cemetery. And it was at that moment time unrolled, flooded the corridors, and washed away the imposter. Hours gone. Urgency. There would be no more summers.

"What are we doing here?" I asked.

She parked.

"I don't want —" But before I could protest, she had already fetched the tulips from the back seat, shut the doors. At a clip, she followed the walking path that was flanked by a procession of arching elms.

I tried to catch up. "Kate!"

She wove her way through the grounds and headstones to a place where the sod seemed to have been freshly turned.

I slowed to a stop and watched her from afar.

She pulled some wilted daffodils from a vase situated near the headstone and replaced with the fresh cut tulips.

I looked back from where we'd come. Retracing steps. I didn't want us to get lost. You need to know how to get home.

Her cotton shift blew gently in the wind. It was at this moment, in that white cotton dress, that I noticed how her body had changed. When? I can't even remember if she had said. Was it a boy or girl? Why can't I remember this?

I ran to her. Ran through her. Stopped dead.

And she looked around as though she'd felt me. "Nick?"

I tried to touch her. But my hand went right through her.

"It's a boy, Nick."

She crouched in front of the headstone and tended to the long grasses as though housekeeping.

Nicholas Takeshi Holt

ニコラス・タケシ・ホルト

August 19, 1977 – February 21, 2020

GHOSTFLY

Seas are wild tonight . . .

stretching over

Sado Island

*silent clouds of stars**

—*Matsuo Bashō*

---

* This Bashō haiku was translated by Peter Beilenson and can be found in *Japanese Haiku* (1955). Do the clouds stretch over Sado Island? Perhaps they arc (but note the loss of an s). Were the clouds of stars silent? Perhaps they were quiet (but again note the loss of an s). In this English translation, the sibilant s repeats nine times, presenting audible rhythm. The letter s beginning each of the four lines and flanking the words *seas* and *stars* presents a pattern. Intentionality in translation or not — there is beauty.

1

MY NAME IS DHIA. The name is a cross between two words: dharma and Asia.

Buddhist. Neo-Confucian. Derridean. The smell of *genmaicha*. My suspicion: that my mother selected bits and pieces of eclectic ideologies throughout her journey and proceeded to shape her own word gods that presided over her speech. As far as I was concerned, it was this principle by which my name came to be. Through bricolage was how she saw and communicated with the world. Incidentally, I should mention that my mother was blind and that her hybrid English was composed of lovely shards of broken. She had an understanding of, if not an empathy for, nature. In her greenhouse she cultivated *gobo*, *gōya*, *momotaro* tomatoes and, encouraged by her father, tried to grow the Kyoto *ujihikari* tea cultivar. Her trees were made up of *kaki*, hibiscus, lilac, and *gajimaru*. The plants seemed to respond to her care and reciprocated with fragrance and abundant growth. This made her happy.

My gawkish father began his circuitous academic journey in earnest in the corn capital of Canada, studying world literature that included everything from Bashō to Szymborska. Then from Taber he crossed the prairie to the University of Toronto, finishing his undergraduate studies; then to the University of Warsaw for his MA thesis work on nation-building through poetry; and then over to Japan for his PhD studies in classical Japanese literature through the Western lens. That's where he found her. He became captivated by my mother, Yuriko Yoshida, and what he called her *shuddering* beauty. My problem? Their love story narrative. I didn't have a chance. No doubt, *my* messed-up love life was result of some kind of cosmological equity system.

He stalked her through a Kyoto temple those many years ago when the tremors shook the city. My father persisted through the seismic rumblings, through the shimmering papered halls, over nightingale floors. He glimpsed her between the antiquated hanging bells that pendulumed with every shake. He was determined, despite the chaos, and the shuffling crowd, not to lose sight of her. I'd imagined he had thought to save her heroically from the Kyoto earthquake. It was amid this confusion that they'd first met.

Though he's become learned about East Asia over time, he never quite understood that cultural essence that is truly indigenous, such as the subtleties of *honne* and *tatemae* or the levels of kinship, ritual, and community. All mystic membranes that connect in their indescribable and immeasurable way, elusive to those who have spent a lifetime wandering the halls of academia. My parents seemed opposite to each other in so many ways.

Yet.

It took her some time to comprehend my father's kind of love. But after a year or so they became so close that she chose to leave her beloved Kyoto for it. She followed him back to the Canadian prairies, where a dream position teaching global literature awaited Dr. Sebastian Mazur at the University of Ezra. For my mother, the promise of a windproof geodesic-domed greenhouse and the assurance of an occasional rainfall. It was here that their life unfolded at a prairie-arid pace. Then the world changed when one daughter came into their lives, then a minute later another.

Jane. My twin sister was unlike me. She was quiet and abbreviated. She possessed an understated disposition characteristic of the monastic. Which, in looking back, might be perceived by some as mild depression. But in typical Japanese fashion, she possessed soft powers. For Jane, a quiet magic prevailed over the loud. As an example, all those pink plum blossom–shaped *mochi* that she made for my funeral were so beautifully civilized — so breathtakingly subtle in their beauty — they were killer. She has a gift. If mochi-making could be considered a gift, that is.

Me? I had my father's social awkwardness, his bookish tendencies, his innate regard for academic rigour to the point of obsession. I was a nerd like him, for sure. But a nerd with a touch of acid.

While my career path was dialed-in (somewhat, now and then, at times, and for the most part), my personal life, as far as my father saw it, was neglected. In particular with respect

31

to books and men. In these departments he theorized that I gravitated toward the *wrong*. A psychologist would have likely found a strange parallel in the *wrongs* related to books and men. My book wrongs were easily cast out. Often if he found a wrong book near his desk he would pick it up, pivot toward the west, and from his chair toss it out of the room like a frisbee. After many a reading session in my father's library, I'd find my Amis, for example, in a messy stack among García Márquez (with the exceptions of *Solitude* and *Cholera*) and the Reachers, orphaned in the hallway.

Wrong men in my life were not as easy for him to cast out as the books were. First in the male bibliotheca was that justice minister, Scott Nevin, whose unethical decision to support the abandonment of the fraud and corruption prosecution against corporate giant Exigis eventually brought upon him relentless scrutiny and resulted in mental breakdown. Next in the collection was Ly Hume, whose research, countless publications from academic to mainstream, through-the-roof citation statistics, and multimedia exposure had turned him into a world-renowned celebrity academic and lent him a polyamorous tendency. After a go at the orgic, I realized we were incompatible — it was hard to picture him as a human, let alone a partner. Then Samuel Proctor, whose Hitler research engulfed him, causing a drift toward Nazi sympathizer. This erratic behaviour, along with his squeaky shoes, was altogether problematic. And, well, I could go on and on. As I say, my father was less than impressed with my wrong choices in the man department.

"Why can't you find a suitable candidate?"
"What?"
"Boyfriend."

His intersection of *candidate* and *boyfriend* was messed. He seemed to have nailed that uncanny relationship between my books and my men, however. Not to belabour the point, but I can't say our discussions weren't rewarding — abstract comparisons of Bolaño and Murakami to Du Fu and Li Bai proved to be engaging discourse. He must have been studying my relationship with men through these conversations. Conversations that inadvertently led him down the trail, then on a quest to define my wrong-man affliction as a literary pattern. With diagnosis detected early enough, my father believed he could cure me. He was certain that somewhere between the books, between the pages, within the sentences — somewhere in his library a formula existed that would deliver a successful love match for his daughter. But he didn't know that true love is neither quantifiable nor quantitative, but rather karmically measured — generally, it's one per family.

As far as my most recent relationship was concerned, the road had gotten bumpy, so a change in journey was inevitable. I was looking for the next off-ramp. Then, as fate would have it, I was murdered on a snowy night in my wondrous glass-globed living room. My body lay beneath that circular room in a bloody heap surrounded by my red-soaked books and papers. Even the rice paper scroll with a

Bashō haiku that hung on the wall about ten feet away had a good quantity of blood spattered across it. I was in the midst of a research series with collaborators from various parts of the world focussing on occupation- and colonization-related attacks on Indigenous women throughout modern history. It was a huge project. Thailand. Myanmar. Ciudad Juárez. Okinawa. A lifetime of mining. The first stage of the project focussed closer to home — Indigenous women in Canada who had gone missing or had been found murdered. Finally, mainstream awareness after all these years of being practically invisible. Since the times of colonization (and arguably when did that ever end?) there had been this quiet undermining, a slow fracking of ancient mother foundations, or maybe a shifting of matrilineal tectonic plates. I was eager to dive into the research and the writing. But then, as I mentioned, I was murdered.

At around eight o'clock my research work was interrupted by a meeting. Well, I ought to clarify that it was a planned interruption. Some faculty members came over to discuss a list of candidates winnowed down as the replacement for a retiring colleague. After fifty years as professor of ancient history and classical studies, the wraithlike David Carruthers was about to realize his dream of retiring close to Campbell River and spending the rest of his life as a west coast ornithologist searching for the elusive Costa's hummingbird. You didn't want to get him started on that bird, though.

As I said, on this evening, we were seeking his replacement. Two internal candidates and one external were being considered. These academics were quite eager to be a permanent part of the institution, as tenured positions these days are like the Costa's hummingbird: elusive and sought-after flutterings.

2

MY MURDER HAPPENED sometime later in the evening, or rather early the next morning. It was surreal. I lay there dying with a perfect view of a bloodied haiku scroll. The poem on the vertical scroll was my father's favourite. As I mentioned, he was a consummate reader who had assembled a decent library. During my undergraduate years, in a first attempt at translation work, I'd scribbled up his Japanese copy of *Oku no Hosomichi* and the English version, *The Narrow Road to the Deep North and Other Travel Sketches*. He didn't know whether to be happy that I was showing interest or crushed that I'd completely destroyed both books — compromised their spines, folded their delicate corners, and Coca-Cola stained the "Visit to the Kashima Shrine" travelogue bit.

Like my father, some teachers are very forgiving and light the flame for their students, and some practice a pedagogy of the oppressed. My father naturally thought he was the sole influence on my interest in Bashō, but it was actually fuelled by my fourth-grade teacher. Miss Newell had assigned a haiku. It was the first time I'd really become excited about homework, and my father's library gave easy access to resources. I channelled Bashō and wrote and rewrote that 5-7-5 pattern. I went beyond in my elementary research and ventured through zones of the city where I probably shouldn't have gone. I wove through the downtown alleys that my parents had warned me never to walk through. I took the path a local girl took when she mysteriously disappeared: from an alley that led into a section of the river bottom behind the arching cottonwoods and thick riparian where drug deals were wrangled and bodies writhed in the sockets of sexual script. In my subversive travels I discovered how the sun fell differently in these dusky-hued places.

Questions arose. Did those people who lived in tents in those bushes feel pain differently? Did they eat different food? Did they have tables to eat the food on? Did they have dishes and forks and knives to put on the tables? Why wasn't I supposed to see them? Did they speak with the same words that I did?

Words.

Words can lead you anywhere, even to places of slow, unknown passage.

My curiosity led me to the top stairs of the Ezra Mission where I was met with a Reverend Jonathan Harms. He was direct.

"This isn't a place for you."

"I-I'm a writer."

"You're a child."

"For school. I'm a writer."

"You have to leave."

"I want to write."

"Not here."

"I know I can write a good poem here."

There was so much silence between us. He stood tall. I stood small. After the silence he agreed to one day. With pre-conditions. I was to stay on that one spot on the stoop. No wandering. No speaking to others. Amid this meditation on greys I watched, listened, drafted haiku, and pencil-sketched dusty men as they came and went. Footsteps. It altered the reverend's day as he felt a need to keep an eye out for me. He brought me hot tea and inquired often about the writing and sketches.

"Do writing and drawing go together?"

"Yes."

"Can they also be separate ways to speak?"

"Yes."

"Which comes first, writing or drawing?"

"They are sometimes together."

"Which comes first, talking, writing, or drawing?"

"They are sometimes together."

"Okay." He was resigned.

In the busy times — lunch and dinner — he came out to make public that he was keenly aware of my presence and that he served as my personal guardian. Reverend Harms even recruited a couple of his trusted regulars as assistant guardians. But guarding me from what? From the guard. One assigned man who was a shade of dust hid beneath his hat and whispered *Little girl* in a low grey voice so only I could hear him. Words can infect. Then when Harms came along, the dust man brightened like someone had switched on a light. They proceeded to chat gaily. Surely Reverend Harms could see through to my guard's grey-fog *tatemae*. But I don't think he could. Some people, I realized, even the perceived wise, cannot see through the *tatemae* of a wily chameleon like a child can.

For me, this was an important day of academic exploration. I discovered that natural light settles differently on some people, mostly men, who don't have food or homes. Sunlight doesn't dance and transform but pools low around the ankles for most of them. That is what my child's eyes saw, anyways. I quietly moved my pencil on the paper. Haiku after haiku. Maybe on that mission step is where I caught the wrong-men disease that my father thought I had. The wrong-men disease latched on to me and burrowed deep. Can you catch such diseases?

3

I WAS EXCITED that Miss Newell had selected me to stand in front of class and recite one of my haiku poems. I delivered with a confidence I'd never had before. "You may sit down, Dhia," she said dismissively.

I had a bad feeling about something but I didn't know what it was. I went back to my seat.

Miss Newell proceeded: "Class, Dhia has demonstrated how *not* to write a haiku." Instantly, I was knifed. No, it was more — a snap. I had done something terribly wrong.

Then she asked Emma Smith to read her haiku. Miss Newell pointed out how Emma's haiku was, in fact, an ideal haiku. It was at that point that Miss Newell somehow managed to tranquilize something inside of me forever. Even class bully Danny Fitzgerald had a sympathetic glance for me. I remember laughing it off, holding back my tears all day by imagining that I was in someone else's skin. That was the first time I'd really pretended not to be me in order to trick my emotions and get through pain. I entered a new understanding of my hybrid world.

Thinking back, I remembered feeling like a little bird.

A bird that Miss Newell had blinded, shot down, and netted. Fish are netted, too. But don't take my word on its own, as it may be defective. Her testimony may be different. In fact, for Miss Newell it may very well have been a non-event.

Another bird that I remembered from then was Michael Jones. Maybe a butterfly. He lived down Starling Lane and took the bus to church when the weather was mild. He was blind. Because my mother was blind, I noticed people who were blind. Precisely at nine o'clock on Sunday morning Michael Jones would emerge from his house with caution. He would make his way past our kitchen window tapping a red-tipped cane down the street as though it were a feeler. He would tap twice to the front, twice to each side, and sweep across, repeat all the way to the bus stop. I remember once seeing some boys cast rocks in front of his path.

The butterfly bird fell.

The boys laughed.

You know something?

My mother had been completely blind since birth. She became accustomed to her world. Beneath the calm, the blind are warrior birds. It's true. She was soft outside, but inside there was incredible strength. Despite the falls, she knew how to keep her soul true. If I needed an extra dose of strength, I held her up as my role model and touchstone. *Sochi* up there, *achi* over there, *kochi* in my heart here. Right here.

Back to the event.

That day, I didn't cry in front of the class. Pretending not to hurt worked. But when the bell rang at day's end, all

I could think about was getting home. Once the bell rang this was my process:

- Did a mechanical dot-to-dot from classroom to locker to school bus with my room as end goal;
- Ran home from the corner stop, freed the brave bird who had, without my knowledge, already begun its leave of absence;
- Burst through the screen door, shoes off, lost pretend-happiness climbing the carpeted stairs;
- Shouldered off backpack to the floor, fell on bed, and cried into my pillow.

My littlest voice wondered if beautiful children were unintentionally treated differently, better, by teachers than plain students. Did the colour of skin matter? Surely it wouldn't. Maybe the dust from the men of the mission had been on me when I stood up in front of class. I hadn't worn my best shoes, either. Surely teachers treat every child fairly whether eyes of blue, eyes of brown, or blind. Don't they? Yes, they do. I knew more about haiku than my teacher did. No, I didn't. My haiku sucked. Yes, that was it.

As I got older, that moment played over and over in my mind and became pivotal. I became transfixed on the translations of Bashō. Though it was my father who presented endless word opportunities, Miss Newell was my best teacher, for she unknowingly served to encourage critical discourse related to inclusion and sparked notions of social injustice. Thank you, Miss Newell. Did you know that the *"seas are wild tonight / stretching over Sado Island / silent clouds of stars"*?

4

SURVEILLANCE.

He parked about a block down the street, in the quiet lane where the fences were high and the thick lilac bushes served to conceal. Around him the unseasonal snowfall powdered, carved, and revised the prairie landscape. It was an uncommon April that couldn't seem to shake winter. A dangling lilac branch scratched at the back window while gusts picked up alley gravel and took random swipes at the car. Nothing new. Ezra-lites were accustomed to those hundred-click winds that pitted and sandblasted their vehicles.

How much longer, he wondered, checking the time on his wristwatch. The ticking sound served to relax him. The spliced Helvetica used for the numbers was a refreshing take on the traditional font. Back when Angler Moss was a master's student, he wrote a paper on the history of basic Helvetica. Now in addition to Regular, Medium, Bold, and Italic, the font family offered typographical options such as Thin, Light, Ultra Light, Condensed Bold, and Condensed Black. Tick. Helvetica Neue Thin, he thought, was his favourite. Not ideal for all applications, but for print, where time could be taken to appreciate the fine typographical line, it worked. But not for television or film. Nor for lower-resolution applications. He wanted to design type when he was younger. Helvetica was brilliant.

Once he became aware of it, the ticking became central. Being both bored and cold, he started the car and blasted the heater to high.

He'd known the meeting was planned for this very evening. It fell into his schedule perfectly. But why so late? He used the downtime to study the lines he planned to deliver to me. Then he took time to go over and over the murder process. It was like cramming for a final exam. But he also used the time to remember the beginnings of our relationship, when all that mattered in the world was the two of us. The laughter, the precious moments, the intention of forever-ness. He shut off the engine when he felt sufficiently reheated. He reached into his satchel, fidgeted some, and found his bag of pipe and tobacco. Soon the car was filled with cherry aromatic. Angler puffed and watched the smoke curl. Beautiful. He became still. Surely, he thought, these people wouldn't stay the night.

Just after midnight, Simon Jones and Lydia Grover decided it was time. Lydia gripped the icy rail, unsure of her weighty step on the snow-covered porch. Joseph Butterfield was last to leave, pulling his favourite Cardinals cap over his forehead and lingering in conversation with me beneath the snow-flecked porch light. Through the gaps in the snow collected on the rear window, Angler fixed his eyes on Joseph and me, sucked hard on his pipe, exhaled.

Some speculated that Joseph was attracted to me. To others, like Dr. Lydia Grover, there was more than just attraction going on. That's the problem with having psychologist colleagues — even those with oblique, multi-, or cross-psych disciplines, as was the case with Lydia: they're always petri-dishing you. In addition to the course work with the graduate studies cohort of eighteen, and her research on the decline of Brony subculture, Lydia seemed to have endless time for gossip. Tending to the analysis of faculty members seemed to lift her spirits.

For the record, there was nothing between Joseph and me. We were simply friends.

"He's the one, you know."
"Nope."
"If I were to choose, it would be him."
"You do not get to choose."
"Why?"
"Because. Hey, I have class soon. I have to go."
"I do, too."
But after that comment from my dad, I imagined. When I happened to spy Butterfield sketching up the whiteboard during his History 3000 class, I imagined.

Simon slowly drove away while Lydia waved.

"Is she watching?"

"Yes."

He cupped my face.

"Still watching?"

"Yes."

"Still?" He pretended to kiss me.

"Okay, they're gone." We laughed a little. Shivered.

"That'll give her something for tomorrow."

"Yes."

"Get inside. Damn cold."

"Yes."

"Thank you for the jam and bread. Reminds me of my mom. Your sister's homemade work, you say."

"Yes. A pastry chef. Her specialty is *mochi*."

"*Mochi?*"

"A Japanese dessert."

"*Mochi*. I'll remember. Let me know when her bakery opens."

"I will."

Butterfield slipped on the icy walk and then did a bit of a goofy shuffle to his car. That last bit for my sake. He got in his Lexus and started it up. While it warmed, he brushed the snow off then scraped the frost from the windshield and rear window. I watched him drive slowly down Starling. Signal and cautiously turn right onto Peacock. The falling snow blinded the red car from my view. I looked about.

White flecks everywhere. Quiet except for the buzz from the street lamps. The peace and privacy of the acreage lots in Starling made the properties some of the most sought-after in the city. Still. The snow fell softly in a world gone small. I shut the flickering porch light off.

5

IN THE KITCHEN, I turned on the light. It crackled and popped dead. Some light streamed into the kitchen from the living room. In semi-darkness I washed the plates of peach jam smears and breadcrumbs, the wine glasses from Quails' Gate. Hands immersed I gazed out the window above the sink. The blizzard.

"Score like this," my sister said holding the hot freestone in the palm of her hand. She manoeuvred the tip of the paring knife through the peach skin. Glints of light danced off the blade as she carefully slit six sections. "Then peel," she said, pulling the skin off to reveal the tender flesh.

"Boo!"

I jumped and turned from the sink. "Fuck, Angler."

"Sorry. Didn't mean to scare you." He snickered at my reaction. "Well, actually, I did." He looked at the light fixture. "Why so dark?" He flicked the switch. Nothing.

"Damn bulb."

He looked at my face in the dim. Searched for guilt, no doubt. May have seen signs of fear rather. Wondered about Butterfield. Jealous and angry at everything. He hated me. But he had his anger in check. I know now that killing me was top of mind. You just don't sit out in the cold for hours unless you are focussed. Fear. It descended first from the ceilings and touched my head.

"What are you doing here? Your lecture. Shouldn't you be in Caulville?" I said, puzzled. "And —"

"Yes?"

"Where's your beard?"

"Time for a change, I suppose."

He pulled off his gloves and managed the fluorescent lamp. His hands were smooth, manicured to perfection. The watch.

"De la Cruz didn't want it anymore. It was from his ex-wife. Sold it to me cheap. I like the ticking."

I took a closer look. "Helvetica."

"Yes, that's right. Good eye."

"Well, it's Helvetica."

"Yes."

"Does it feel different without your beard?"

"Yes, it does."

He rubbed his face where his whiskers once were. Angler had dimples that parenthesized the corners of his mouth. I should have filled the space with something like *You look good clean-shaven*, but I didn't. Angler Moss knew how attractive he was to women, and to men, too, for that matter.

His head of too-thick hair fell in a perfectly controlled mess —
calculatingly dishevelled, as my father had noticed upon
meeting him for the first time. My father had always been
suspicious of perfection. Angler could enchant anyone in
the room, especially my sister. Yes, my sister adored Angler
for a time. The graphic design connection. Even my mother,
who was a good judge of character, was at first bewitched by
Angler. But there was something that my father saw. Another
wrong one. Red flags.

"You don't like him, do you?"
*"I don't know him." My father bit his tongue, turned back
to the Books section of the* Globe and Mail. *His lack of
candour with me — or more precisely, his silence in this
moment, and in many subsequent others in relation
to the strange and contradictory behaviours that he
perceived in Angler — was something my father would
always regret.*

With or without scruff, Angler's face with those eyes of slate
blue mesmerized. He was even more physically attractive
without the beard, if that were possible. "It feels good," he
said rubbing his chin with the back of his hand. His look
drilled with challenge. I remained unresponsive. Such trail-
ing off marked an ongoing motif in our declining relationship.

"I forgot my PowerPoint file. I'm lost without it. It's on my
memory stick," he said quickly. "Besides that, I forgot the
author's copy of my book. That one that I use as my lecture

resource. Invaluable, as I have all the places highlighted that I want to read from in it. For my lecture, I mean, necessary," he said, over-communicating.

"That's a four-hour drive here and back. Likely longer with the snowfall. That's —" I was careful not to say the word *crazy*. So I said hushed, "That's *insane*." Only a slightly better word choice than *crazy*. Fear had fallen to my ankles and pooled. I'd fallen off the tightrope so continued. "I thought you knew that lecture well enough to have it practically memorized."

"Visuals," he said, his eyes boring through me. "Essential. There are some overseas delegates attending — if they don't have a grasp of the literature, the images will help."

"Semiotics."

"Yes."

"Yes, I suppose." Since when was he so thoughtful about such things, though, I wondered.

I put the remaining bottle of wine in the fridge. Thought that moving my feet might shake off the fear.

Angler awkwardly advised, "You shouldn't be drinking wine, you know. You're apt to be sick again. Ah, let me guess, Butterfield the Great brought it."

The moniker Butterfield the Great was a sign, an argument originator. I remained silent.

Angler's agitation rose and words tumbled out like misshapen cubes. "Well, he doesn't know that you're allergic to some wines. Does he?" He searched my eyes for some sort of betrayal. "Does he? Fucking pretentious idiot."

I sensed an impending bout of the fury that I'd become familiar with in this house, under this roof, exclusively my experiences. I threw on my armour, remained unresponsive, and steered clear of direct eye contact. Soon, the bristly energy went down another road and, uncharacteristically, diffused. Angler quickly regained his calm.

"Well, I hope you came to a decision on the tenure track." Through the snowfall, from his hiding place across the street, in the alley, from the vehicle, huddled in the driver's seat, cocooned in the down-filled parka, wrapped in a Burberry that protected his clean-shaven face — from this place through a frosted window he saw and had waited for the search committee meeting to adjourn. His head had filled to overflowing.

"A gathering," I offered.

"A meeting."

"Yes."

"You ought to be more precise, Dhia." Angler's face suddenly softened from its grimace and screw. "There's something." Random. "I still love you." There was an eerieness about him and about the whole moment. He waited for response.

"Sss —" I said after time. I made the weird *sss* sound in order to prevent my mouth from spouting something I might regret. It was ridiculous. After *sss*-ing I awkwardly continued to wash the rest of the dishes. Fear pooled and tension paced.

I reviewed: what had attracted me to him in the beginning? Mostly appearance? Was I that superficial?

I assessed: yes. Angler Moss was the most beautiful man I had ever seen. I had a weakness for beauty. Yes. After a string of bad choices in men, I guess I was bound to either win the man lottery or lose the whole kit and kaboodle — the latter being one of my father's favourite idioms. Personally, I'm partial to *the whole shebang*. Either way, Angler and I did have some things in common at the beginning, didn't we? Well, it seemed that way. Maybe when you want to be in love, you try hard to find those things. You see, imagine, or construct likes that reveal themselves later on not to be. Then after time, the *tatemae* collapses and you fall off the rails, and you fall and fall. I think I told you what *tatemae* means, didn't I? It's your public face. When that falls off, you are left with only winter. Maybe my father was right about my attraction to the wrong men being a disease. Or maybe, in my own defense the easiest explanation: I was only human.

A stretch of silence.

"Well, I better get my book and memory stick." He made his way through the obstacle course of video bags, umbrellas, tripods, then dashed around my scatter of Indigenous Studies texts — Gunn, Bastien, Wagamese, Ahenakew, Halfe, among others — toward the desk drawer and found what he needed. On his way toward the door he embraced me and then awkwardly crept his hand around the back of my neck, slowly pulled my hair down from the topknot, and then viciously drove down the front of my blouse. He pulled me close. I smelled that sweet cherry tobacco. An attempted kiss. Life and death, the four seasons, the dynastic cycles of Imperial China, the Spanish Influenza, the Black Plague sped through my mind and informed me that this wasn't uncommon, our relationship was one of those variable natural patterns of unfolding broken dreams and promises. The strands from my topknot waved gently across my face with his breathing. The top button of my shirt dangled by a thread. There was a time when the smell of his face, his breath, his hair pleased me. He was the beauty of a husband, then. Now, after only a year, everything about him repulsed me.

"You're a bitch," he whispered with a smile and a strange glint. He gathered up his gloves, his author's book, his memory stick, random papers, and a communications journal, squared the stack, and stepped into his boots. The opening and sudden slamming of the door sent a final chill throughout the house.

I finished cleaning the dishes. Threw on a hoodie.

Still wide awake at two o'clock in the morning, I decided to work on the video component that contributed to both my research and my online Advanced Indigenous Literature course. I'd hoped the work would bring a sense of calm that would help me sleep. The segment of my presentation on Halfe's "Nōhkom, Medicine Bear" served as the Canadian contribution to my research project on Indigenous women worldwide. The camera was clear across the room, ensconced in the corner, already set to the perfect angle.

I pressed *record* and scooted into position, clipped the mic onto my collar, and began to read:

A long day's work complete,
Nōhkom ambles down the stairs,
sweeps her long skirt behind her,
drapes her paws on the stair rails,
leaves her dark den and the medicine powers
to work in silence.

That was it. I couldn't recite Halfe's poem from memory. I needed the book and it was somewhere in the mess near my feet. I began to rifle through the stacks of papers. Suddenly I heard the sound of the door blinds shudder ever so slightly and the door hinges creak the way they did, with that high note upon opening and low one upon closing.

I froze and then slowly rose from the heap of books and took a tentative look around the ugly faux-Doric column into the entryway of the house.

We'd found it at an art exhibit that featured abstracts of Greek architecture. Angler had spoken with the artist. "Would you be interested in a commission?" he had queried.

It was the one hideous aspect of the interiors. If we ever sold the house, I thought, that. That. A deal-breaker.

Then a thump sounded from somewhere in the house.

Unfamiliar sounds in my home during the daytime usually passed without much concern. But unfamiliar sounds at night unnerved me. I glimpsed at the security alarm beside the mantel and wished it had been activated. We'd discussed it several times, even had a password chosen. What was it? *Morse1837*, yes. Angler's idea. He had thought the association to his new media discipline was clever.

I reluctantly scanned the room. If I visually skimmed without focus, without too much thought — well, surely ignorance would bar the netherworld from crossing over. However, I did listen carefully. The familiar boom of the damper echoed. The heater sequentially ignited the burners. Sounds that were dim throughout the day were now present. The falling snow on the windows and siding battered. The clock ticked. The weatherstripping flapped at the screen on the door. Finding measurable explanations for the mysterious house sounds, I let out a sigh of relief.

I decided to stack the books and tidy up a bit before going to bed. In my back and forth process of moving the books to the desk, I glimpsed the mirror over the fireplace and in the hall a blurred reflection of what I thought was a shadow. I turned away from the mirror to look around. Nothing. Nothing but a phantom. But a phantom is a ghost, isn't it? And there, I thought too much on it. My heart pounded. My mouth dried. The shadow brushed across the wall again. I noticed small puddles. I dropped the books and stared in terror at the figure down the hall leaning against the bedroom door frame. The casual body language terrified me. It read: *I've done this before, I've hurt birds.* I could see the Cardinals cap tipped down. In that tiny fraction of a second, I felt myself literally perched between earth and nothingness. I knew without a doubt that *this* — whatever *this* was — was soon to be over, and that *this* would not end well.

"Joseph? What are you doing here?" I said, trying to maintain calm. I smelled cherry and my confused senses swirled. The figure emerged from the darkness of the hallway, raised his head, and pulled off the red cap. I inched toward the front door. He continued to advance.

The room suddenly contorted.

"Angler?"

He looked different.

"Yes."

"What are you doing?"

"Nothing."

Can the physical features of a person change so much that they look like they're wearing a mask when they're not? His warm gaze quickly turned to ice. His skin creped. The bright eyes became dull. I couldn't breathe because the air had changed, too. I attempted escape. He hooked me around the waist with his arm.

"Fucking prick."

He laughed a bit.

I punched him solid in the face as hard as I could. Unsure of where it landed. But it did land. He punched me in the stomach, my glasses fell off, and I folded. I saw a glint. The metal caught the reflection of the softbox light. *It was raining slivers of glint.* The sounds became painful. My ears heard things as I struggled. Something hurt and I wasn't sure what Angler was doing. I wanted to try to reach into that place he was deep in and reset him. I wanted to say his name. But I didn't want the word to be last on my lips. So, I whispered Bashō. Drifted. I cowered from the blows and soon the blows didn't hurt, and soon the sounds couldn't be heard. I just stared up at the domed skylight, my favourite feature of the house and began to sleep. *This is it*, I said to myself. Three simple words that summed up a life and all the memories that encompassed it fit into a moment of *this is it.*

Don't cry, I said to myself.

I'm not, I responded.

Don't be afraid.

Then there was such a beautiful silence, you know. I didn't think that silence had those beautiful sounds and those glorious colours. But guess what? *Silent clouds of stars*, it does.

6

THE SNOW FELL AND FELL. Angler Moss hoisted the bloodied garbage bag over his shoulder — any evidence was in that black plastic bag, all drenched in my blood. He carefully tucked the Cardinals cap upside down near the base of the lilac bush in front of the house. He figured it would freeze in place there, to be discovered in the next day or so. He made his way to the vehicle where he neatly pulled off the gloves, threw them into the bag of clothes, and cinched a very tight knot.

The dash clock lit up 2:33 a.m. and even though late, a few houses had their interior lights on — not surprising as the gentrified Starling Glen was inhabited by a diverse community of driven artisans, farmers, and professionals. The community once Ezra's red-light district. The neighbourhood included the Singh family who lived across Starling Road and a little to the south toward Peacock Boulevard. The Singhs were a large household with a burgeoning international weaving, pottery, gemstone, and metallurgic business called Indus Valley Civilization Inc. They had become successful, it seems, due to their strong business connections overseas and their institutional ties to museums, universities, and libraries. The grandparents, Zah and Mary, did a daily walk to the Starling green strip and simply sat at the bench for a time watching the owl family in the tall pines. The Singhs had brilliantly integrated the image of their grandparents into their multimedia global marketing strategy. Over at the right-hand corner of Peacock were the Thompsons. They owned a three-generation family farm known as Making. The Thompson men were in and out of the house to the fields, day and night, seeding, irrigating, harvesting, adapting to conditions. Rumour had it that they were planning new crops such as chia and cannabis, and their grandfather was not having any part of non-traditional seeding on his land. Tonight, lights were on. The Thompson women, meanwhile, were tailors and weavers who had an online business called Working Class, ironically appealing to the higher income household — their sophisticated twenty-first-century marketing strategies appealed to a credentialed target market.

Meanwhile, further along Peacock, Drs. Ship Larson and Annari Ketlar, professors in the Faculty of Education at the University of Ezra, collaborated on their neuroscience in education research. We knew them as acquaintances, saw them at institutional functions, and read about their work and awards now and then in the University of Ezra publications and communications material. They were part of that faculty that everyone on campus envied — a nationally respected teacher preparation program where all the students and the faculty seemed oddly utopian. Ship and Annari had one child of their own and four adopted from different parts of the world. Three children had moved away. They were teachers. Two of the children remained at home, one studying to become a teacher while the other required twenty-four-hour care. The Ketlar home was always awake. Angler saw that the Singh house, along with the Thompson and Ketlar homes, was still, even at this ungodly hour, abustle. That's what he was counting on.

He drove for a bit and then parked the leased Lexus for about fifteen minutes near the intersection of Starling and Peacock in clear view of all three homes. He even honked a couple times. While idling, he went over the next steps, his trip back to the University of Caulville, and delivery of his morning lecture. Considering the poor road conditions, Angler calculated being back in Caulville just before dawn, ready to present on the subject of communications.

Soon. Over the past years, Dr. Angler Moss had delivered his *tour de force* lecture flawlessly with only minor tweaks. In a few hours he would include a new introduction that touched on ancient oracle bones and then a skim through Kublai Khan's brilliant communications strategies, which included a relay of mounted riders and the establishment of standardized roads. He would present the newspaper format that included Stead's sensationalism; referenced Bell and Vail; cited Hall, Kress, and van Leeuwen; and investigated the introduction of digital communications technology into the mainstream. He would speak of the almost overnight obsolescence of analogue (even noted light tables, darkrooms, four-colour process, X-ACTO knives, Letraset along with the humble burnishing tool); and media scrambles, acquisitions, and mergers that significantly changed the communications landscape. Finally, the capstone of the lecture would explore social media, the ushering in of quantifiable metrics, and end with the future of communications. It was impressive. Angler's presentation would then dovetail into an audience Q&A — which, incidentally, was always lively.

With the storm easing, the gentle fall of snowflakes was illuminated by the cast of the street lights — a descent of white against the winter's night. In the distance there was a faint spread of aurora borealis. Noting the time, he was confident as he drove through the quiet neighbourhood. At precisely eight thirty a.m. he would be standing in front of the U of C theatre lectern. In a few hours, the packed gallery of over three hundred communications and new media professors, communications experts, and students from all points across Canada would be waiting on his keynote speech with devices charged and ready. The IT folks would have the streaming already in progress and moderators would be poised to address the in-person and online audience. But what truly mattered to Angler was that his carefully engineered alibi was airtight.

After the wait Angler drove the shiny red Lexus down Starling and took a right, careful not to slide into the curb. Anticipating a white-knuckle trip, he proceeded with caution to Highway 2 en route to Caulville. *In a world of one colour, the sound of the wind.*

7

I WOKE to a dark and still mid-morning. The kind of dark and still that comes just before a rainstorm. Then it did. Rain, that is. The rain came down like a cloud of a million slow spears. Needles cast long, fine filaments angling from the sky. Yes, it rains in this dimension just as it does down there. In fact, there isn't as much difference as one might think. One thing is apparent, however — time is different. Rain falls slowly, and with that one can observe the way the light embodies each strand, the way it impacts a puddle, quakes, and concentrically ripples. The action catches the light differently with each ripple. Time copes with colour differently, too, as amber and indigoes, for example, present in an unpredictable manner due to the nonlinear aspect. Colours? They linger and bleed. Time seems to slow the inhale of beauty — or what I perceive to be beauty. The stretch of sunlit rain, for instance, seems to hold in its seemingly small vessels stories that you have never heard, particle voyages that are multi-directional, carrying a cargo of riches you can't even imagine; and then when they fall, they touch my skin, my eyelids, my tongue.

This state seems to exceed any earthly fantasies of heaven. I am cloaked in the rain's sublime beauty as I become privy to the collective rain stories and the way they heal my glaring wounds.

8

MY FATHER WAS in the kitchen ladling an egg out of the ice bath. He broke the top of the egg with a few taps of the back of the teaspoon and eased the cool silver between the white flesh and the brown shell. It was all about timing and patience. He slid the spoon around the egg and quickly scooped it out onto the toasted marble rye bread. This was his favourite part of the process. It felt so rewarding to extract the egg whole and leave the shell intact. Magical. Then he broke the egg with the spoon, allowing the yolk to ooze over the toast. "Perfect," he whispered. He twisted the pepper mill over both plates and set them on the book-strewn kitchen table. He pushed aside translated copies of the *Shiji*, the set that he wanted to integrate into his life and have suffer through the stains and tears, bumps and bruises. The other set pristine and untouchable on the top shelf in his library. He scampered to the sunroom.

"Hey then, Yuriko," he called out. "I think —"

At that moment the phone rang, and he retreated back to the kitchen. "Hurry, *tabenasai*," he said before picking up the phone.

"Dr. Sebastian Mazur?"

"Yes."

"Are you the father of Dhia Mazur?"

"Yes."

"Sir, my name is Sergeant Stafford Finn. I'm sorry to say I'm calling with bad news."

———

THE OFFICER WAS slow in speech. Words drifted about — *DNA, autopsy, evidence, crime scene, lab reports.* These words were overshadowed by the word *homicide. Homicide* ran right through my father's entire being like a knife. The officer asked my father to identify my body. My father wasn't listening, only desperately hanging on.

"Yes."

Trying to regroup, he put the phone to his other ear as if the story would change.

"Baz? Who is that?" My mother dragged her fingertips across the kitchen countertop, garden glove limp in hand.

"You are certain? I mean —" He could see my mother approaching. Closer.

"Yes."

Closer.

9

I FELT THE RAIN thicken the bookish air of this old library. My new home. Ladders led up to shelves and shelves of hand-picked books: some new with crisp pages and spines of integrity, some beloveds weathered and misshapen. There were graphic novels, fiction, non-fiction, pop-up books, poetry, academic texts, and even the personal diaries of Darwin, Polo, and Hawking. I was granted power to decipher, as well, which meant entry into a world of writers whose original works I could never have read before, such as Sima Qian or Bashō. This place was candescent with natural light. My idea of heaven was right here, and it left me utterly breathless. Outside, a strange sight to me: absent of wind, the rain fell straight. In Ezra I'd become accustomed to a whole repertoire of winds. There were winter chinooks that polished the sidewalks and roads with black ice; summer hurricanes that would corkscrew semis into ditches; and fall storms that could uproot centuries-old pines and cottonwoods. The differences here were subtle but wondrous. Windless. The sound of rain. Resplendent light. The books.

10

"WEATHER'S BEEN CRAZY, hasn't it?"

Nothing.

The officer was silent as he drove to the station, cast quick glances at his back-seat passenger.

My father sat solemnly. His mind raced back and forth in time from when I was a baby to when I was a teen, then an adult. He wondered if I'd experienced much pain. Where the pain had occurred. How long I'd been in pain and what level it had been. He wondered about the details of my protestations, the manner in which I'd been killed. Try as he might, he couldn't stop his imagination from blooming like a cancer. It was set loose to delve further into the possible physical and mental anguish I may have suffered. His brilliant and inquisitive mind — a liability. It was apparent to me that rather than serving as an asset, his fostered and rigorous habit of critical thinking was now a handicap.

He tried to engage with me. He tried very hard to connect to the universe through the hidden powers of telepathy even though he didn't believe in that sort of thing. Nevertheless, I heard him. He didn't even have to try too hard. I heard him. Dhia, are you there? Can you hear me? *I'll see what I can do, Dad.* Are you okay? You promised me you'd share your fishing trip in further detail, he thought, regretting not having spent more time in conversation at the last moments together and only glancing at the gallery of fly-fishing photos. I'm going to hold you to that. I'm sure to see you again, bounding through that old front door with the sun at your back and ready with another story of the day, talk about a book you were reading, or enter into conversation about research that intrigued you. There are too many things left unfinished. Our plan was to fish along the Crowsnest this summer. You can't possibly be gone.

"Front and centre, Dhia, front and centre. Cast out now."
I followed his instruction, and to my wonder, I had caught my first fish. That was when I was ten years old.
"There you go."
"I love you, Dad."
He didn't hear me.

For my father, my death signified the end of one way of life and a jagged transition to an unknown other — and every frail step from this point on, every sound, image, thought, and breath, was going to be fraught with pain. For as much as he loved me was the extent to which he would ache for me. He couldn't help but deny the loss and resist the change.

The pattern of comfort with a child had shattered. Those rainstorms we enjoyed, the laughter in the house, those conversations about wrong books and wrong men, or my space in his library in relation to his. The rain fell with an urgency.

A girl was walking down the deserted street. The top of her hood flopped down over her eyes. The rain soaked her inadequate garb. He thought for a moment. *Dhi* — he mouthed. My father put his hand to the window and turned his head, trying to look beneath her hood. Just for that moment, I made the girl turn, too, and through her eyes I could see through the dark tint of the ghost car window. Our eyes, my father's and mine, I mean, locked for a split second and then I fell out of her.

"Dhia?"

The officer side-glimpsed my father. "Are you okay back there, Mr. Mazur?"

"No, thank you," my father said incongruently.

The officer remained calm and looked straight ahead again through the clearing of the wipers. The rain began to pick up tempo.

My father felt the vehicle shake from the intersecting mid-city track spines. The old coal town grids remained part of the roadway, holding up traffic now and then for flour cars and even causing a few traffic deaths. He watched familiar landmarks and their darkened corridors and intersections pass by in the gloom. The dingy old mill, Overpass #1, Overpass #2, Emmett Card's Dodge Chrysler dealership, the first shopping mall ever built in Ezra, the northside Safeway converted into the Garfield Hockey Arena, the

Ninth Avenue bridge and traffic circle, the roof of the homeless shelter down the slope near the old train junction, McDonald's, Tim Hortons, Walmart, Chinatown, and the three-storey boarding house. Arteries led out to the endless spill of fields — wheat, canola, potatoes, mustard, barley. Where urban ended and rural began in Ezra was a mystery.

A pit of wallow. He had plunged into utter darkness and was trying to climb out, tried to gain a foothold on reality by tapping into the formula, or at least the acknowledgement of a pattern of familiarity that he could grasp. Unknowns circled predatorily, ready to pull him. As he watched the rain streak the window, he hung on dearly. For he had glimpsed what he was looking for there in the rain. He saw it and embraced that trace transmission of the familiar. *A cold rain. And no hat.*

STAFFORD FINN SAT across from my father. The folder of photos between them. "These are images of physical aspects that may assist in identification," he said in his gravelly voice. "Thank you," my father replied.

Dispassionately, Finn took a long hard look at my father. He assessed and quickly made a comprehensive mental list. White male between fifty and fifty-five years old, a little over six feet, slight build, messy dark-brown hair greying and thinning at the temples, wire-rimmed glasses a little crooked, dressed classically, ivory shirt, belted charcoal trousers, dishevelled due to his distraught state, and likely mildly sedated, from the look of things. Probably couldn't figure out what to do with a power tool or a baseball glove if his life depended on it, either. Middle-class academic lifer, socially awkward, physically limited, navel-gazer, almost always insecure beyond self, institution, and home.

"Your wife couldn't make it? How's that?"

"She can't see, Sergeant Finn."

"She can't see?"

"Yes. She's blind."

"Oh, yes. Um. Sorry. Gotcha."

After all these years, his profiling skills were top notch, but he still, and had always, needed improvement in the area of soft skills. The lack of soft skills was where Finn failed as a detective of distinction. For without those soft skills there was a gap that greatly impacted his ability to assess others. What he saw in front of him was a nebbish man — but what he didn't know was that sometimes still rivers run very deep and the careful reading of rivers, rather than the dismissal of them, takes a detective from average to brilliant.

Finn was nearing forty years of service that had spanned the British Columbia Rockies and across the prairie provinces. Homicides were his specialty. On paper, he should have long been in an administrative role and ready to retire with a big pension. Off paper, not even close. After the *disappearance* he couldn't stay in one place too long. Especially near Prince George, especially anywhere near that corridor. He caused an epic schmozzle trying to resurrect the E-PANA investigations, which led him to *nowheresville* Ezra. Promotion: highly unlikely. Wives: four. Daughter: vanished. Destructive habits: yes. Good friends and colleagues: none.

My father methodically went through the collection of photos. Finn was a chronic shaker, and he caused the table to shake, too. My father looked up from the photos.

"What is it?"

"You're shaking the table."

"Oh, sorry." Finn pushed his chair away from the table.

"Thank you."

There was an image of a raised three-inch scar on my left thigh from the fall I'd had as a toddler. He'd always told me it was a good luck butterfly symbol. The next photo was a close shot of the small mole on my right earlobe. Another photo was the small tattoo at the nape of my neck that read *Bashō*.

"What do you think?" I pulled my long cola-coloured hair in a twist away from the nape of my neck revealing the tattoo.
"It's awful."
"I like it."
"You've made a mistake."
"No, not a mistake."
He went back to reading his paper. Then looked at me over his wire frames. "No need to concern your mother about this."

The Ezra Police Station was quiet. All but this little room occupied by Stafford Finn and my father. He carefully stacked the large-format photos, placed them back into the folder, and took off his wire frames.

"Is this your daughter?" Finn rocked forward and sat at ninety degrees.

My father closed the folder. "I want to see her."

"It's not advisable. Moreover, it's not allowed." That was the first time he had ever used that word, *moreover*. He thought it would be a good word to use with a professor.

"Not advisable?" My father queried with fear as he ran through the scenarios of why it was *not advisable, not allowed.* Was she torn apart?

"Is this your daughter, Dr. Mazur?" Finn said again, reaching for the folder of photos.

"Let me see her."

"Dr. Mazur, there's a process. They're presently investigating the circumstances surrounding her death. We're looking at this as a homicide. So in order to maintain the integrity of the body, forensic pathology suggests, or rather insists, against it."

Out of character, my father picked up the chair and threw it with unexpected strength. Finn ducked and it hit the two-way mirror. "Let me see her," my father yelled.

Unfazed, Finn pressed his cigarette out with a twist in the corner of the table. My father leapt at him and attacked with a possessed anger. He struck Finn in the mouth, then thrust his right fist into the officer's left ear. Finn staggered. Wiped at his face and saw the blood smear on his hand. "Aw, shit." Finn had the patience of a man who had been in too many fights and the confidence of a man who'd won most of them. He was sure that rabbit punches were all my father had in him. He waved an *I-got-this* hand toward whoever was on the other side of the two-way mirror.

"Calm down, Mazur. I don't want to hurt you," Finn said firmly. He tried to manhandle my father into docility, but it didn't work. Another fist to Finn's rib cage. The sergeant groaned and caved from the blow, and he glared at my father with some surprise. Finally tired of the jostling and taking the body hits, Finn punched my father square on the nose, felling him immediately. "Fuck the soft skills," Finn muttered, shaking out his fist. He picked up the upended chair with one hand and righted it back in place. He then picked up my father and sat him down. "Is this your daughter, Dr. Mazur?"

My father, doused in sweat, glasses smeared with blood, nodded and then spine-arched a dry gag.

"Behind you, Dr. Mazur," Finn said, scratching his forehead. He rocked up to a stand and tucked his shirt into his pants. Then he returned to his chair, leaned back, and tapped his shirt pocket feeling for cigarettes.

My father found the waste basket and proceeded to retch into it. He wiped his mouth.

"You don't mind, do you?" Finn mumbled taking a step toward my father, cigarette dangling from this mouth. He snapped his fingers at the lighter a couple times before it sparked. "I just need a puff or two. Give you a chance to simmer. Bad habit. Picked it up when I was fourt—"

My father turned and took a swing at Finn. The cigarette flew from his lips, the Zippo fell to the floor, and the big man went down. "Fuck *moreover*," my father said and retreated to his chair.

12

THE EARLY-MORNING RAIN was an encore of the previous night. "Cobblers' knives," my dad said as he stared out the kitchen window at the rain.

"What?"

"Just commenting on the rain, dear."

"Oh."

After my death, some words and their rhythms impacted my mother and she often wished she could unhear them. The television and radio remained either off or low in the distance. She began to realize that hearing words like *homicide, investigation, mystery, bloody, brutal, custody* felt like jabs to her belly. She refrained from listening to certain audiobook genres like mystery, thriller, and crime. After a time she also avoided listening to newscasts. All her senses were grieving.

"Hm."

"Hm?"

"They have someone in custody."

"Who?"

"Joseph Butterfield."

"Oh."

"He's been made a formal suspect."

Joseph's was not the name my mother had in mind. They both knew who it was. "Doesn't sound right."

"No."

"What's he like?"

"Who? Butterfield, you mean?"

"No, the man leading the case."

"Oh, Finn. Just a man."

"Oh?"

"Nothing stands out about him."

"Just a man," she echoed.

"You wouldn't like him," my father said. He glimpsed the tomatoes on the counter. "But he's competent."

"Is he?"

"Yes."

"Oh."

"What are you planning for the tomatoes?"

"I have no plan."

13

AND BASHŌ WAS a warrior once.

A scent of chrysanthemums washed through me as I lay on the window ledge and gazed half-lidded at the ceiling painted with ancient Buddhas. Now faded and distressed. The cat found a new position at my feet.

14

WEEKS AFTER MY DEATH, the sun unleashed an awakening to the prairies. As far as my family was concerned, the good weather arrived specifically to defy their time of mourning. To them the brilliant day was disrespectful to those whose loved ones had recently departed (or, in my case, been murdered). To the sun, it was as though the April blizzard and my murder had never even occurred. People went about their usual business amid the splendour of the day. Seasonal routine was restored. Gardening, the mowing of lawns, outdoor landscaping projects, children's laughter, family picnics, patio parties, civic holidays, camping trips, and vacation plans — my parents resented the sun for this show of joy.

"They insist we go on a walk with them."
   "Soon."
"They're worried."
   "Yes."
   "Soon?"
   "Yes, soon."

Before my death, my parents were avid walkers. In fact, as my father would say, they were *bonkers* about their outdoor walks. My mother loved every season for one reason or another, and my father took pleasure in describing the nature walks in detail to her. At the break of dawn on Sunday mornings they would circle around Henninger Lake with two other couples. The 3Ms, they called themselves — the Makarenkos, Millers, and Mazurs. Colleagues. Anna Makarenko was in neuroscience, doing Alzheimer's research, and her husband, Phillip, was a retired school principal from Taber. Tim Miller was a sociology professor whose brilliant sub-theory on Marxist literary rendition of the proletariat and bourgeoisie had made him a sought-after lecturer even after his retirement. Like my mother, Paige Miller loved to garden. Unlike my mother, she was once a prostitute in Amsterdam. Of all my parents' friends, I liked Paige the most. Her laughter infectious. The 3Ms would often attend university functions as a group — plays, ballets, donor galas, dinners. Angler and I would attend some of these same formal functions. But it seemed my parents and I would rather be fishing, hiking, camping, or enjoying a good book. And Jane? In every instance she'd rather be in the kitchen baking.

"The 3Ms can wait, then."

"Yes."

"Too soon to socialize."

"Too soon."

Another ritual that my parents took pleasure in was the Farmer's Market held from May to October at the Ezra Pavilion. Again, my mother noted the aromas and the textures of the produce, and my father described the visuals to her. Though walking with the 3Ms was on hold, they did venture out of the house to the Farmer's Market.

"Will there be a lot of people?"
"We'll see."
"You look lovely."
"Thank you."
"A new dress?"
"Yes. Jane picked it out."
"It's perfect on you."
"Thank you."
"The Nakayama family is here. They're waving."

Nakayama's Nursery was run by an elderly Japanese couple. They offered plants unusual to the area such as *shishito* pepper, *takenoko* bamboo shoot, sometimes the *kamo* eggplant. Recently they had launched a green tea business influenced by their daughter, Rika, and Finnish son-in-law Teemu. The smells were so distinct. My mother was reminded of Kyoto and the family tea farm.

Some of the regular exhibitors were there. The New York Hutterite Colony displayed their perfect elephant garlic, first pick of strawberries, early-season pickling cukes and dill. Xavier Greenhouse presented their tomatoes and

crucifers. Zozia Franc was there with her homemade per-
ogies and cabbage rolls. Empty booth spaces were set aside
for the much-anticipated Taber corn.

"Jane is busy at her booth."

"Does she need help?"

"She is managing."

"What does she have today?"

"Poppy seed rolls. Maybe walnut. I can't tell."

"Mochi?"

"Yes."

"What kind?"

"Looks like kinako and daifuku."

"Busy, you say?"

"Yes."

It wasn't the same this spring, for obvious reasons. When
they encountered friends and acquaintances, conversation
about the circumstances of my death was excruciating.
Understandably, the tragedy seemed to cause some people
to act quite strangely around my parents. *I'm sorry to
hear,* they would say and become flustered and continue
awkwardly; or there would be a complete avoidance of the
subject; often they seemed to be in a hurry. The most painful reaction was when acquaintances would do an about-face
when they saw my parents. The spoken word proves inadequate and inaccurate in conveying sympathies, sometimes
resulting in unintentional and irreparable gaps. When a

child is murdered, relationships can be strengthened, and they can also be lost — as my parents are discovering.

"What did she say?"

"She said at least you have another daughter."

"Oh."

"Hm."

"She doesn't know."

"I shouldn't have stopped to listen to her. That was a mistake."

"A mistake to stop and listen?"

"Yes."

15

SILO. It's a funny word. Say it several times and it sounds odd. Etymology from the Greek *siros* or the Basque *zilo*. Either way, a place to store grain. To a degree my parents chose hiddenness to buffer the pain related to losing me. Loss: a permanent puncture to the spirit and soul. Murder: a word that fractured their senses. Both words changed the open-hearted and hopeful way by which they had approached living. My father began to sleep in his library surrounded by books that were stacked and spread-eagled on the floor, on his desk, on his chest. Even my previously evicted *wrong* books were now included in this chaos. He desperately tried to find a way, through rigorous scouring of words, sentences, and concepts, to navigate through this time of pain and confusion. My mother spent all her time in the greenhouse with her plants. For her, the inexplicable cruelty of the event of my loss was broken down into focussing on quietness: dirt preparation; moving the quietness: managing the water and nutrients; aligning the quietness: keeping the stems and arteries of the plants straight and open; and equalizing the quietness:

being careful not to privilege the plants that were the most beautiful or the most thriving. Rather, she looked to assist the plants that were in distress. She transformed the act of gardening into a deeper practice of self-care.

My sister dealt with my death in her own way, too. Jane channelled the loss into productivity as she focussed on her bread-making experiments, perfecting her *mochi*, the world of coffee beans, and the branding aspects of her new shop. She wanted to set herself apart from the other bakery cafés.

My sister had a background in writing and design. This was something that she had in common with Angler. In the beginning they would talk about the pre-digital history of design, the overnight demise of analogue in print and television. For a couple of short-lived months before my death, they brainstormed about preliminary branding and communications strategies for Mochi Café.

After my death she began to work with a fury, scribbling into the night. Soon logos, physical store layouts, signage ideas, video storyboards, content development, and online commerce endeavours began to stack in little piles on her desk and throughout her kitchen work area. The ideas were beautiful and the journal-style sketches as part of the shop's strategies began to evolve.

The typographic concepts emerged. Serif or san-serif? Mochi Café in Times New Roman Bold Italic, then in Helvetica Neue Thin. The clean sans serif seemed to breathe. Then she tried it in Moon Flower, which seemed whimsical, but she thought too trendy. She sketched countless studies.

Then frustrated and tired one night, she sketched the name ANGLER in Helvetica Black, pressing the Blackwing, and scribbled until the tip of the pencil snapped. I felt my throat constrict as I watched her memory unfold.

"You won't tell anyone."

"No."

"Good," he said, releasing the grip on her neck. She was tangled. "Otherwise —" He threw her on the bed.

I was privy to a deeper layer of those I had left behind. A part of them I couldn't know before. I could see bits and pieces of each of their private struggles, but some of their thoughts and memories were impenetrable. It scared me how much I truly didn't know about them. Humans wear masks. How much broader my misunderstandings and misperceptions now seemed. Most of the issues didn't seem to matter. But my perspective had changed. To them, they had shaped a lifetime of making the things that mattered to them complex. To me, I could see the world and the vast timeline of existence. I could see how each one of them was only a speck of dust in the grand scheme of things. When I lived down there, the small family with our creature comforts looked like a cohesive unit. From up here, my loved ones looked like a heap of repelling fragments.

I sat in the alcove of the tallest window of the library embracing the wreckage below. I watched them go about their lives, and I missed them. Their delicate shells clung to their cores only by virtue of habit.

16

LYDIA GROVER HAD remastered a Dhia and Joseph story that spread like a virus throughout campus. The dubious nature of the story was sadly the linchpin of its fascination, and for a brief moment a peculiar *schadenfreude* derived allowed some hearers to feel better about their own lives. Dr. Angler Moss was Grover's victim in this tragedy. It is at this point that I turned my attention to a place I'd been avoiding since my death.

Beneath the crimson swath of early-morning pastoral, I saw the silhouette of my killer rise over the hillock. The intoxicating beauty of the land could make anything in creation look exquisite. On first sight he was the poster boy for all those mythic hero motifs. Classically sculpted, he portrayed a noble air, possessed squared shoulders, and held an assured stance. His thick hair was a tousle of chocolate brown and his eyes glistened like blue jewels. It was impossible not to notice his outward spectacle. But first impressions fade, and it is hard for a human to conceal their inner workings for long. On matters societal, while Angler's circles seemed rich in diversity, they were in fact monochromatic. While he seemed charismatic and generous, something imperceptibly unsettling existed behind his smile. The truth of the matter: he was confined to a private island of one and within existed a powerful callow. No one ever came close enough to understand how effortless it was for him to slip into the dark coordinates of his world.

Angler Moss was returning to our home in Starling Glen from his Saturday morning communion with the vast spread of the coulees. It had been seven weeks since my death. Because they confidently had Butterfield in hand, the investigators never really pursued other possible suspects. It was evidently a classic open-and-shut case. Angler was clean off the hook.

He pondered the last year and considered how he would go forth with the rest of his life. Wipe the slate clean, he thought. His jealousy of Joseph Butterfield, his anger with me, all his transgressions — these were clearly the chief factors for the regression of his hostility. Angler thought he would be granted some semblance of salvation now. How he reconciled his fleeting noble thoughts with his past was a mystery.

To the Crow. *In the eyes of fish.*

17

MY FATHER SAT at his desk in his library. Gear sprawled.
When he tied, he seemed unbound by the known order. What
I mean is that when I watched my father creating his flies,
he seemed to shut down the world and go inward. He would
spin strings and feathers like he was the wind. He became so
focussed that there was nothing but the surgery of fly-tying.

"*Wrap the yellow string around the wire along the hook
shank then up to the curve. You see?*"
"*Yup.*"
"*When at the curve, wrap over and over. Build the body up.*"
"*Okay.*"
"*Watch the tension.*"
"*Like this?*"
"*Yes. Remember the nymph tails, these tapered biots.
The goose's first flying feathers.*"
"*Okay.*"
"*Biots are delicate. Careful not to damage when you pull
them off the stems. You could destroy them.*"
"*Forever?*"
"*Yes, forever.*"

I watched my father combat despair. Even the rudimentary was agonizing. Fingers tangled, he couldn't get into that fly-tying pocket, and in a short time intentionally tore the biots off the stem and angrily pushed the feathers and hooks off the desk. Even the vise fell away. "I am sad," he yelled. "I can't fucking get in anymore." He surveyed the fly-tying materials scattered about the floor and sprinkled on top of his sprawl of books.

18

UNIVERSITY COLLEAGUES were called upon as witnesses. Lydia Grover shared all she knew and even embellished about campus trysts and collaborative research projects. Her accounts led to the *coup de grâce* — she admitted to witnessing Joseph and me kissing on the porch. This act of mischief on our part would result in profound consequences. In the courtroom while she was on the witness stand giving testimony with clarity and force, I hovered over her shoulder and whispered, "You truly are a gifted fabulist." I wondered if at that moment she regretted the strange joy gained throughout the process, or perhaps she heard me. She underwent a peculiar change. While on the stand she lowered her head and in an uncharacteristically quiet voice managed, *That's all.* From that moment on, Lydia Grover never spoke a word about the murder, the trial, or Butterfield and me.

The damage was done, however. There were sightings of a red Lexus in the early morning hours; the Cardinals cap was discovered tucked under the lilac bush; Butterfield's fingerprints were throughout my home; and it seemed the murder weapon was found. Contextually, the knife wove ever so nicely into the Butterfield family owning a taxidermy shop. In addition, a clerk from Haliburton Guns and Sports in the outlying town of Taber told the court that over the years, the Butterfield family had purchased many such tools for their shop. **MURDERER.** The *Ezra Herald* finally had a story worth printing on the front page.

Imprisoned. A thick curtain of darkness fell. Joseph Alexander Butterfield was in custody and had gone through the intake process. Removed from society. Whether in the classroom or incarcerated, he wasn't the stereotypical placid university professor. In minor and junior hockey years, Butterfield was a defenceman and due to his size and tenacity had been groomed as an enforcer. He'd been in a few brawls, and in custody the bear-baiting that circled reminded him of those times on the ice. He'd already had a bit of a tussle with the arresting officers, then a skirmish with a guard. But this fight culture was no game. There was no referee and there was no way out. I saw him being led from one spill of darkness to another, past predatory shadows, and finally to a holding cage. This was a world different than that of a tenured professor at the University of Ezra. There was noise of metal against metal as the mesh gate opened to the clanking of locks, clanging of chains, and an atmospheric hunger.

The evidence against him was strong and interrogations were intense. Over and over he was held under question.

While in his cell, he retraced the evening just to be certain without a doubt that he was, in fact, innocent. His life had become surreal and he wasn't sure of anything anymore. It was like the recurring dream he'd had all his life — the one where he was freefalling without a place to land.

After time he attempted to solve the murder. He'd made some preliminary notes and scrawls during the trial that later served as a resource for his portfolio of sketches and essays. Evidently, the multimedia work that he created while imprisoned helped keep him sane. Here was the outline to his research:

1) Draw the material evidence presented;
2) Compose renderings of each witness in the court-room along with their testimony;
3) Script in great detail the meeting held at my house prior to the murder;
4) Storyboard scenes from the moment he arrived at the meeting to the moment he left.

The light in his soul dimmed. He could now see shadow-things dwelling in the darkness of every turn. Some hunched quietly in the gloom, and some, more sinister, emerged. It was the ordered work of trying to solve my murder that served as an anchor for Joseph Butterfield. This deconstructive process seemed constructive in offering his addled mind something familiar to latch on to. In this new world, maintaining the familiar was the key to sanity.

19

It was a Friday evening. The library was quiet.
He came up behind me as I pulled Bashō from a shelf.
"Good choice."
His face was beautiful. I simply stared.
"Sado. The island of gold —" *he said.*
"— and exiles," *I said.*
"Fan of Bashō?"
"Yes."
Of course, he knew my answer would be yes.
"Name?"
"Dhia. Your name?"
"Angler."

20

ONE DAY ANGLER DECIDED to get away from Ezra and headed west toward the Crowsnest Pass. All he sought was a short day trip. The prairie topography unfolded before him and he thought that a phrenologist would have a field day here. He drove with the window open; the wind masked over his face and the heat miraged before him on the highway. He emptied so completely he felt as though he was rising, and decided he was in prayer. It occurred to him that just maybe he was finally beginning to understand the prairie pathology. Some invincible power he was part of. After all, he'd gotten away with murder.

The sun was liquid gold on the prairies. Each patch of farmland displayed a different earth tone. One after another.

He pulled over to a side-out, unfolded the accordion map, and saw the scribbles all over it. He recognized my handwriting and put his glasses on in order to study the notations. In pencil, I'd marked the reserves in western Canada that the map had overlooked. In fine lines I'd attempted to draw the isolated roads that led from the reserves, the lonely Greyhound bus routes. On the Trans-Canada Highway I'd highlighted locations where Indigenous women had disappeared, noted which reserve they had come from, and the year in which they went missing. I focussed on Highway 16 between Prince George and Prince Rupert. That accordion map was a resource for my academic research. His day trip westward was now two hours long and already he was becoming road weary. The heat made him sleepy. The expanse of the sky, the solemn farmland, the solitude — he saw it all as lonely. This trip wasn't at all what he had thought it would be. He should have known. In addition, tractors, threshers, semis, and all sorts of vehicles on the highway posed a navigational challenge for Angler. Sometimes he'd find himself lost even within Ezra for hours at a time. Sometimes he'd come out of a shop in the mall and, disoriented, head in the wrong direction. It often took a while for him to grasp the concept of directions — north, south, east, west. He had only ever driven on Highway 2 between Caulville and Ezra, never veering off to points west on his own for fear of getting lost. Today, he had wanted to escape from Ezra and he did for a while. But now he had decided it was time to turn around and go home. He got out of the vehicle and stretched his legs, assessed his surroundings, and then did an arbitrary wander to a nearby field. He didn't stray too far.

As far as he could tell by looking down the long stretch of road, there was no one around for miles. Something he'd always wanted to do: he did a 360-degree spin in the vast canola field. "I'm free," he yelled upwards, coughing a bit. I advanced toward his shoulder as best I could and quietly said, "Free." I felt he had heard me and acknowledged my presence just as Lydia Grover had when I'd whispered in her ear on the witness stand. Yes, I interfered, but no one had stopped me. Perhaps interference is tolerated rather than considered a violation.

There was a peacefulness in the heart of ag country. Then a northerly gust picked up and I quickly snatched the map from Angler's fingertips. I stopped the wind and held the crumpled map in the air for a good ten seconds. Nothing moved. The suspended motionless map was surely black magic above him. From up here I heard Angler's heart pound with fear as he stared at the map pinned to the sky. Then as if the world exhaled, I let the wind take the map across the wheat field. Admittedly, mischief.

Then a chill. It was as though with that act I'd allowed an opening of darkness. There was something in the air, a faint smell of burning sweetgrass. Rustling. Angler's head pitched to nowhere in particular — ears perked; listening, listening. He'd heard the rumble that I'd heard and felt the presence that I'd felt. It began in waves. First there was drumming low and visceral; then there was the sound of pounding hooves. A mist billowed out of the opening and spectres of mounted warriors emerged. Their war screams a symphony of terror. They were hunting for monsters. Angler ran; the monster ran. He ran through the field. They were furious on his heels. Angler screamed as they overcame him. They ran right through him, leaving a cacophony of scents that infused him, a fear that pierced him to the bone. Then they were gone.

Angler ran to his car, returned to Ezra.

21

SHE TOLD ME that there was power in scents, that aroma could be as deadly as a weapon or provide elixir. I interpreted: between the two extremes lay a vast cascade of experiences.

I grabbed a pineapple with my mittened hand and held it in front of her. "What's this?"

"Pineapple."

I held a small carton of strawberries to her face.

"Strawberries."

"Does rain have a smell?"

"Yes."

I looked outside the grocery store window. "Snow doesn't have a smell."

"Yes. Snow is my favourite smell."

"What?"

Jane gazed out at the window.

"What is it?"

"Snow."

"Snow? This time of year?"

"They're huge."

"Tell me."

"The size of hands. And they're not really falling. They're sailing."

My mother went outside.

"Mom?"

"Yes."

"Snow!" Jane laughed.

My mother held her bare arms out, palms up, and face to sky. "Snow."

22

MY FATHER WAS FIXATED on Stafford Finn, began to peck away at him. For the tenth time in a week my father made his way downtown and up the unnaturally wide steps of the Ezra Police Station. They were the kind of steps that needed a lot of thought to climb as one didn't know whether to take one long stride or two small steps per scale. Both awkward. After time, my father developed a method.

"You can't keep coming 'round here."

"Why not?"

"No point. We've got the man who killed your daughter."

"You've got the wrong man."

"All evidence says we got him. Witnesses in the neighbourhood saw his red Lexus, his Cardinals cap was found, fingerprints on the wine glass, the murder weapon. Jesus, how many times do I have to go through this with you, Mazur?"

"Until you get the right man."

"You're wasting my time."

"Butterfield is not the man who killed my daughter."

"Yes, he is."

"In your gut, you don't believe it."

"I —" Finn knew it didn't feel right. Butterfield didn't feel right. Then from behind the desk he rose like a mountain.

"Please leave, Dr. Mazur."

"I won't."

This time, Finn was prepared for my father to lose it. He pulled up his sleeves and stepped around the desk toward my father.

"Snow."

"What?" Finn tentatively turned about. He was astonished. Large white flakes fell like pages from the sky.

23

FIVE YEARS HAD PASSED.

"Hey."

"No preferential treatment, huh, Professor?"

"Yup, you're here forever."

"Get used to it."

"Yeah, welcome to hell."

It took five of them. Fists punched, feet stomped, tattoos revealed. Butterfield lay bloodied in a dim corner of the Ezra Remand Centre. His large figure crumpled like a car crash, his left leg numb and mangled. He hadn't even been segregated yet, or administered for file into the general unit, and already some of the other prisoners had targeted him for my brutal murder — an inner sanctum social system where a savage panopticon strategy was understood. In here, the epistemological and dialectical methods are fucking useless.

Encultured.

"This detention centre will not tolerate this kind of behaviour. Do you understand, Butterfield?"

"Yes."

"I'd advise you to dispense with how you lived out there and learn how to live within these walls. Okay?"

"Yes."

The director of the Ezra Penitentiary tapped his pen on the metal table in the dimly lit room. "Be assured, you are in a well-oiled correctional facility."

"Yes."

Remember who said what, and when. Dialogue was different in this world. Words here were euphemisms and weapons. Concepts such as engagement, diversity, cohort still applied. For his own safety, Butterfield was quick to assess his surroundings by recognizing some social parallels to the halls of academia. Who said what, how they said it, and who listened. Race relations and classifications. Those who were silenced (either forced or by choice) helped him understand the leadership and hierarchical structure of the pre-trial, term, and tenured population. Everyone was going through their own personal hells. He realized his ability to bring critical thought and assessment to this new environment might help him adapt and survive at least until he fit in. He began to study every nuance of incarceration — even and especially the sounds. Fist on flesh, aching moans, reading footsteps, silences, and commotions out of place.

He'd landed on the other side of the coin. On this side there was an industrial nocturne soundtrack that played over and over. Butterfield had no choice but to submit to the dysfunctional orchestration.

24

THEY BASKED in the sunny spot of the greenhouse, my mother and her persimmon tree. She felt around the rim of its terracotta planter, measured the moisture of the dirt with her finger, and then poured water accordingly. Only the one tree to care for now. Since her decline, she'd delegated care of the garden to my father. *Decline.* Sometimes a word, the way it sounds and the way the letters look (in this case somber), is exactly what it means. The word *decline* means deteriorate or degenerate, and it does look like it would mean something grave. It's the *de.*

At first it was little more than abdominal cramping. Then she was diagnosed with diverticulitis. She was given a two-week prescription of a quinolone antibiotic that she didn't take to well; within days perforation was discovered. It was a miracle she recovered from the septic shock. As a result, her legs became weak and her thinking and standing became increasingly problematic. It was a mystery, according to the doctors. She had contracted some sort of neuropathy after my death. More and more she relied on the wheelchair and subsequently her mind fell in and out of *decline.*

"How does the garden look today?"

"Beautiful."

"Is that all?"

He was filled with guilt. "Well."

"I may be fading. I may be blind. I know the garden has died."

"Yes. How did you know?"

"It began to smell and sound different. *You* began to sound different. You're a terrible liar."

"Yes."

A warm breeze swirled about. Dead leaves and blossoms milled about the unused paths and along the cinder-block beds.

"Why didn't you say?"

"Because."

The mournful sound of a distant train. Birds. A soft patter. Then more came down.

"I miss Kyoto, Baz."

"Tea, then?"

"*Hōjicha.*"

"Okay."

"Take me out."

"It's pouring."

"I don't care."

He pushed her out into the open, to the middle of the backyard. He spun her around as the rain fell bringing with it a delicate scent of persimmon.

25

ANGLER NO LONGER WANTED my personal belongings in the house. It had been five years and he didn't want reminders triggering memories or guilt from the murder. He didn't want to glimpse my clothing or Bashō, or my research — nothing that would remind him of that night. He had considered having all of it taken to the Ezra landfill. But he didn't think that would be a sensible idea. That kind of act was bound to show up on social media and resurrect the story. One night, after making a dent in the Quails' Gate *gewürztraminer* and while uncharacteristically grappling with his scattered emotions, Angler packed my belongings. The next day, suffering from a hangover, he called Gentle Hands Moving Company and within a day was guiding them through my items. They efficiently finished the work of packing and labelling.

"All these books?"

"Yes."

"What about this electronic stuff?"

Angler had received a substantial grant for brand-new tech equipment. On his wish list were twenty Apple stations and an editing room, a personal max-capacity MacBook

Pro, a DJI drone, a virtual reality classroom kit, a couple mirrorless Fujifilm cameras, long and *bokeh* lenses, plus the total Adobe Creative Suite for twenty-five users. Virtually anything he wanted the department would finance. With this in mind, he considered all my research tools dated. Besides, everything that he ordered for the department was essentially for the classroom and for his own personal research, too. Out with the old and in with the new.

Without prior notice, the moving company delivered twenty-one boxes to my parents' house. Angler was relieved to have it all gone. Finally, with the removal of my belongings, his life was restored to some semblance of order. With me completely purged from the house he could move on.

Weeks passed into months. My family avoided the work of sifting through those boxes. Every now and then either my father or Jane would quietly go downstairs and open the door to the spare room to the stacks of boxes that held my things. They wouldn't touch anything. They just wanted to look at the boxes — be with them. Jane would sit cross-legged in the room with the boxes and just breathe. The room smelled faintly of me: a melange of things from childhood like spring and winter; a coulee walk; a prairie rainstorm; and Waterton Lake laughter — my mother would attest that laughter had a scent. To Jane the room sounded softly like me: the riffling of pages; a pencil scribbling on Strathmore; Ryuichi Sakamoto lilts; curiosity — my mother would attest that curiosity had a sound.

One day Jane pulled up the flaps of a box near the room's entrance. Books. Then on another day she opened another box. She realized that the boxes were mostly filled with books. Hearing the boxes being moved about, my father wandered downstairs. "Is it time to go through them?" "Yes." Jane dragged three boxes out of the room. "Why don't we start with these?" she said. "Maybe three piles. One for keep, one for give away, one for throw away." "Okay."

My father found a box of essays and papers related to my studies. He'd always thought my cross-disciplines of Indigenous and Asian studies unusual. But I saw a significant relationship between the indigenous prairie and islandic cultures: the discovery, conquest, and colonization; the parallel of waving wheat fields and ocean waves; the hegemony that filtered into the school systems with similar penalties for uttering the origin languages; the residual impact of violence upon women; the tangled interpretation of oral culture translated into written form; and how their histories were written largely by the dominant voices in history. I truly believed in this research and had a lifetime to study it. Then a change of plans. I was killed.

My father glimpsed one of the papers in the stack of papers:

Even though Thomas King and Richard Wagamese are contemporaries writing about First Nations

experiences, they represent story in different ways.
Their personal journeys and those of collective
others uniquely impact the lens by which the story
blossoms — manner of expression, measure of words,
the people these words represent, and consideration
of origin stories. All of these peripherals seem to
contribute to the way story is approached in their
writings. King utilizes multi-platforms in delivery
and also seems to have successfully converted
Nigerian Ben Okri's words into a tagline: stories
is all we are. Whereas Wagamese says that "you
humbly tell a story, and the story gives you the tools."
It seems King believes the story is in control of us,
while Wagamese believes that the story as compass
and collaborator offers us the tools necessary to
control, deliver, and then repair connections.

He began to pore through my research one paper at a
time as though he had only now discovered that I was not
simply morally compromised by choices of wrong men, but
was in fact, a full-fledged, multi-faceted human being on a
promising scholarly trajectory. His own untapped research
foci from his years as a young academic came to mind and
he was invigorated. Here in these papers and words he
was introduced to a daughter whom he didn't know. The
Indigenous writings of Ahenakew, Halfe, Bastien, Gunn,
Wagamese and a good collection of global writers such
as Hämäläinen, Trouillot, Césaire, Fanon, Ishihara, Asato,

Chinen, Yamazato, Smits, Wolfe. He even found the dog-eared Bashō that had gone missing from his collection so long ago. He wept at seeing my collection of books. He wept out of guilt for not truly *seeing* me even though he was closest to me. I wished he wouldn't take that guilt up. Because it turns out we can never truly know one another no matter how close we think we are. Then his tears turned to bittersweet joy.

"Dad, what should we do with all of this?" Jane held my laptop.

He wiped his eyes quickly with his sleeve. "Um. What is it?"

"Everything's tangled. Adapter." She rummaged. "An old set of headphones."

"Anything good?"

"It all looks past lifespan. Maybe?" She pulled out the Canon DSLR and plugged it in. "Looks like this stuff hasn't been touched since Dhia —" The blanks in sentences where *died, was murdered,* or *was killed* should be inserted were now part of their understood language. "I think he just threw everything in here." She proceeded to fiddle about with the jammed memory card door and noticed the scratches on the LCD screen. "I could use this for multimedia stuff. I wanted to make some online video tips for the bakery website."

"Take it."

"You sure?"

"Yes."

"Not working. Maybe broken."

"Battery?"

"Um. Yeah," Jane said, releasing the battery from inside the bottom of the camera.

"Is there a charger in the box?"

Jane rummaged again. "No. Doesn't look like — oh, wait. Yeah. Here it is."

"Charge it. It probably hasn't been used since —"

My father took a stack of essays upstairs to the kitchen table. He made himself a coffee and continued to read.

26

SACRED TIMES, places, and things. Do you have them? Do you even know you have them? Down there, I quietly, secretly, even unknowingly had them. It's only now that I, with crystal clarity, understand the significance of *sacred* in a world of chaos and urgency. On Sunday mornings, I used to do this: I used to write with coffee by my side. I'd set my place at the imperfect pedestalled kitchen table that my father made — perfect by way of its imperfection. Three small daughter plants that my mother had potted from her Kyoto tea plants were semi-circled on the periphery of the table. The sun fell on that table in a strangely humble way. Which is to say, the table seemed to have a long-standing affair with the sunlight, same time, same place. That's partly why that place felt so good. I'd then set my stack of books on one side, coffee on the other, my laptop before me. It was here where my *sacreds* convened to write a sentence.

27

JANE WANDERED UPSTAIRS after some time. "I'm going, Dad. I'll come over tomorrow to help with sorting the boxes. There are clothes. You won't know what to do with them."

"Sit and have a coffee with me," he said, looking at her over the rim of his reading glasses. "What about that battery charger?"

"Oh, right." She went back downstairs and came up with battery and camera in hand. Loaded. "Let's see if this thing works."

Jane began to take a few photos of Dad. "Go take photos of your mother," he smiled. "Not of me."

"She still sleeping out in the back?"

Dad nodded. "Go take some of her. I'll only break the camera."

Jane rolled her eyes. "Original." She managed a smile and continued to test the camera, taking random photos with flash then without. "It looks like it's working. There's a bit of a hairline crack. But —" She toggled the ISO, f-stop, shutter speed settings, played with the zoom, and then switched to video mode. *Fast-forward* working, *Play* not working, *Rewind* working. *Play* again. Working. Suddenly there I was. Jane was startled to see my image on the camera, hear my voice. That lingering pain of loss that she had grown accustomed to surfaced quickly. It was a clip of me reciting a poem or presentation or something research-y. She didn't want to watch. But she knew she had to. Watch, rewind, watch, repeat.

A long day's work complete,
Nōhkom ambles down the stairs,
sweeps her long skirt behind her,
drapes her paws on the stair rails,
leaves her dark den and the medicine powers
to work in silence.

My father lifted his glasses atop his head. He saw my sister was visibly distressed. "Jane?" He laid down the papers. "What is it?" Took off his glasses. "Is that Dhia's voice?"

In the background of the clip, Jane saw something in the shadows that I hadn't. There was an image moving behind me as I read from my pages. She began to realize with horror that my last moments alive were caught on the camera.

[shuffling sounds then silence]
"Joseph? What are you doing here?"
[The figure comes into the light]
"Angler?"

28

"LET'S JUST GET STARTED. Petra said she'd be a little late."
Angler pulled the syllabus up on the wall and scrolled down
to the discussion points. "And Henry's sick today." He was
halfway through the Cinema and Politics course and enjoying
this particular MA/PhD cohort immensely. They were eager
and engaging. "So, the assignment was to watch Cuaron's
film *Roma* and write a twenty-page essay referring to nation-
alism and citing earlier readings. As you know the deadline
for your assignment is today. Submit online by midnight.
Also, submit a hard copy in the mailbox near my office."

Stafford Finn led half a dozen armed officers into the
classroom. "Dr. Moss?"

"Yes."

"Dr. Angler Moss?"

"Yes. I'm in the middle of a class." He flinched uncharacteristically.

"Yes, you are."

"How dare you impose. You can't —"

"I can and I will," Finn said. "You're under arrest for the
murder of Dhia Mazur, Dr. Moss."

Angler was confused. "But Butterfield —" His demeanour changed immediately. "I said, you can't come into my fucking classroom and —"

"We can."

"You have no cause to —" Angler's fury shot up. The students seemed to fade into the walls. Cell phones collectively tapped.

"We have cause."

"Gentlemen?" Finn nodded to the officers. "Remember, be concise." He thought Baz Mazur would have liked that word, *concise*. "We have a lot of work ahead with Dr. Angler."

"Get your fucking hands off me."

It took four of them to wrestle him to the ground and cuff him. They filed out down past the faculty offices in the B wing of the Arts and Science building. Lydia Grover leaned out the door. She opened her mouth to speak as they passed her; there was nothing but a whisper that no one heard: "But he's normal." She glimpsed Angler exude a wicked face that couldn't be unseen. Desperately trying to appear boyishly *normal*, he recast Lydia a mechanical *go-to* laced in charm. *On the monkey's face, a monkey's mask.*

She retreated into her office, closed the door.

They proceeded through the Bronsky Honour Hall walkway, across the Student Union atrium, and past the open area food court where a group hush was followed by social media synchronicity. Then through the double doors to the campus quadrangle. Eyes peered out of the hundreds of office windows at the business at hand centre stage.

119

There were two officers in front, one on either side of a hand-cuffed Dr. Angler Moss, and two behind with Stafford Finn at the heel.

29

JOSEPH BUTTERFIELD was found innocent, formally exoner-
ated, and awarded substantial compensation for wrongful
conviction. Butterfield was a survivor. He had become a bit
of an urban legend. Angler Moss? Guilty of murder.

He stopped for a moment. One last rustle from the leaves.
After giving the foot some time to rest Joseph pressed
onward. The rain began to fall even harder.

Upon his release from prison, the University of Ezra
had offered him two positions: Associate Dean of the Faculty of Arts and Science, or his old position enlightening
undergraduates on Canada's more silent past: Residential
Schools, the Japanese-Canadian internment, and immigrant histories. He asked for a combination position,
and without hesitation it was granted. He was more than
qualified. There was rumoured inside chatter about a path
toward presidency. Really? The old Butterfield would have
been enthusiastic about such a possibility. But now? The
power squabbles, funding cuts, and default hypocrisies?
No, thanks. He had a newfound urgency; he wanted to

continue to work with the future — those brilliant young minds.

Honne. The north wind picked up, pierced and drilled down, around. It was the kind of wind that finds you, the *real* you. Exposes and leaves you. Vulnerable.

He pulled his collar tight around his neck. Shelter. The cold weather seemed to aggravate further. He held tight to the handle of his cane and stumbled into the warmth of a charming corner shop.

Peaches.

Green tea.

Freshly made sweet bread filled the air.

She had just finished making *mochi.*

THE
RYUKYUAN

琉球人

1

始まり

begin: *hajimari*

Refrain from movement.

He lay still for a while longer. In his feverish misery head ached. It was an unusual autumn morning and there was unusual movement outside his house — sounds of excavation. At this time of the year road repairs traditionally snaked in an absurd labyrinth from one end of the city to the other. Rattled nerves. One detour led to another and another. The City of Ezra was once again desperate to patch up its infrastructure in time for the back-to-school season. The sound of men directing one another. *Here. There. Stop.* He wrapped the pillow around his head and rolled toward the digital clock. At precisely seven o'clock a.m. and in accordance with Ezra noise permissions, the jackhammering began.

He glanced up, out the window, noticed the feathering grey clouds shapeshift with fury. Crows inked the elm branches. What was with the crazy weather lately? Apocalyptic. Yup, it truly was the end of the world, he thought as he proceeded parenthetically to assess the historiography of dystopian books he had read, games he had played, and movies he had caught on Netflix over the last years — bleak endings all. He hoisted himself out of bed and sat at the edge for a while scratching at his scalp, his beard, then his crotch, and surveyed the bedroom half-lidded as he did every morning. *These days.* He was tired of waking up depressed *these days.* But *these days* were tough. He knew that time would pass in that philosophical way: better yet, in a *Farmer's Almanac* way. Whichever and whatever, there was no denying that life was hard now and then. Best to semi-anesthetize as he couldn't find an anchor if he tried.

Sounds. He *could* hear a tap-tapping echo from the vent. Simplicity was his go-to pattern now. As secretary of the invisible thing, he listened. Maybe a skill to nurture while depressed, listening. It wasn't construction noise. Rather, it had begun to rain. Another hobble to contend with. *Stop*, he heard from outside. *Pity. Reset*, he heard from inside. Despite what he saw as a dismal personal life of late, having recently returned to his mother's home (the "post-farmhouse" as his dad had lightheartedly referred to it), his curriculum vitae served to remind that at least his career was on a somewhat positive track. Hard work was in his blood, and genetics was keeping him glued together. The rain began to fall even harder, the drops becoming larger and larger.

Cze Wozniak was a third-generation Polish Canadian immigrant rooted from people who worked the fields and mines, prairies and foothills. He came from labour diaspora, from men as large as oak trees and from ample women of the horse. He came from a mighty revolutionary bloodline. But words? He didn't come from words. An elementary teacher had recognized potential in his words and in his ability to shape them into sentences. Soon books filled his bedroom, then the house, and he was taken from the world of the field and replanted on a different path than that of his father, grandfather, and great-grandfather.

The academy took him but could not fully colonize him. While gaining a major in communications and new media with a minor in history he had enriched his studies with courses on economics and international development, studies in colonialism with focus on the *post-* and *de-*. Dissidence. Ancient proletariat blood continued to flow through his veins and pump his heart. The fact was that he defaulted slightly to the left, yet he was fascinated by the beauty of the word and its power to revolutionize. He had taken a few of Baz Mazur's English classes on the Polish Nobel laureates in literature: Milosz, Szymborska, and a more recently adopted obsession still on the fence, Tokarczuk. His journalistic style began to take shape. Cze emptied his head and watched.

Through the window he studied the drama of backlit clouds as they roiled and churned, then he saw the sky open and drop the payload. *Hail.* The jackhammering stopped. The ricochet began. Golf ball–sized hail bounced off the ground, pummelled the house. He found Oe on the bed atop the crumpled blanket, randomly opened, and read *You need oxygen...* That Bird needs oxygen. He fell asleep again.

Over these last months, Cze had been given some interesting assignments — *legit* journalistic assignments. He had reported effectively on high-profile provincial political scandals and the national cryptocurrency mystery that broke from an acreage just outside of Ezra. He had managed to establish an audience. The *Ezra Herald*, happy with their fledgling reporter and eager to secure him, rewarded him with a top of the line, state-of-the-art Nikon complete with accoutrements necessary for multimodal work. He could tell a print, video, or online story from his home or wherever in the world the company sent him.

Cze used the camera in off hours to study the composition of daylight, nightlight, and artificial light. Mostly he would go find some obscure scape to shoot. It fascinated him that the human eye sees the world differently than how the camera sees it. Management wasn't looking at it quite so esoterically. They needed someone to infuse a critical edge into their regional delivery. So, in addition to the rest of the multi-tasking, they offered Cze the role of administering their Twitter account. To reflect the increased workload a substantial increase in pay was promised. Four months in, however, and that promise had yet to be realized.

So. His professional life at least *seemed* solid. His personal life, by contrast, was a shitshow.

His now *disappeared* wife had carried out a scorched-earth departure strategy: accounts emptied, credit cards maxed, a counter-productive online effort to destroy his image, furnishings of any value efficiently swept away one morning by the Gentle Hands Moving Company — leaving husband and boy war-torn. All struggles such as the post-secondary debt, his son's medical bills, and his own mild addictions intensified, and new ones began to emerge like monsters especially those concerning mental health. He had weaknesses. Old habits circled. It was just a matter of navigating temporary turbulence in *that* part of his life.

He hoped the company would soon fulfill its promise for a raise in pay, for he desperately needed the money. But he was grateful to even have the job. It was the work part of his life that gave him normalcy. *Still, yet, however, but,* and *though* branched at every turn. Something wasn't right. There was this weird nebulous *thing* looming. It, the *thing*, was nothing tangible. But his gut instinct told him that something else was definitely about to happen (as if he needed another *thing*) — he couldn't tell if it was good or bad. He leaned toward bad. But maybe, whatever this *thing* was, it could wait. For at the moment he was busy struggling with an early autumn cold accompanied by clusterfuck sneezes that triggered mind-bending headaches, a runaway wife setting landmine after landmine, and the boy. *Thing. Thing. Thingly thing.*

Hryvnak's Russian History 3000-level course. It was in this class that Cze and Maddie first met. She was quick to raise her hand to speak. Cze wished he had not sat beside her. She was *that* student. After the first class he resolved to find another place to sit. But he was late to the second class, and the only desk left was that same one next to her.

Maddie struck up conversation with him and after the first few weeks she grew on him. She wasn't as annoying as he had first thought. Beneath her large-framed, thick-lensed eyeglasses, Maddie Messier was actually really pretty. Soon he found himself looking forward to their conversations.

They agreed to partner on the class presentation assignment. She proposed incorporating something visual. She turned out to be a cinephile. Maddie was into the black and whites that he couldn't bear.

"Have you seen the doc *Russian Ark?*"

"Nope."

"Set in the Hermitage. Russian imperial history. We could entitle it '*Russian Ark*'s Treatment of History in a One-Take Sequence.' Hm?"

He rolled the corner of the syllabus. "Nope. Couldn't get through a one-pager on that. Never mind a twenty-page collaborative effort." He was thinking the intersection of two Russian authors. Which two didn't matter as they were all good. That's what he proposed to her.

"I don't have time to read *Anna Karenina*," she argued. "I have five classes this term, and you only have three. I don't have the time to immerse myself in Tolstoyan contemplation."

"I could focus on Tolstoy and you on Solzhenitsyn."

"Same problem. I don't have time to —"

"Solzhenitsyn was very critical of Stalin. You seemed interested in Stalin a couple classes back."

"I know."

"Went to prison, forced into labour camps. Underdog hero figure."

"Yes."

"Won the Nobel Prize for literature."

"Let me think on it."

Cze whispered, "He studied mathematics. He was a math teacher."

They went on to earn a grade of 97.5 percent.

They also participated in the student union magazine. Cze was editor, which he saw as a way not only to apply what he was learning in communications but to explore voice. Maddie served dual roles — financial officer and advertising sales — which she saw as a way to be near Cze. The two became inseparable.

After graduating with great distinction in Education, Maddie was sought out by several public school districts in the province. She chose a position with the Ezra Public School District teaching at elementary level. After juggling a position as college instructor and freelance work in journalism, Cze began to miss the focussed research and rigour of formal studies. With Maddie's support he dropped the college work to pursue graduate studies. They had a perfect arrangement and within a couple years became parents. Life was — refreshing.

The three went about. Idyllic life.

"What would compel a Comm grad student to pursue research with a corvid strand?" It had been a constant source of comic banter throughout the years of Cze's study. "It makes no sense."

"Crows. Brilliant," said Cze. "Experts in communication."

"Crows?"

"Bird gods."

"Really?"

"Yes. Striking subjects for the photographer, sketcher, scribbler. Haunting in black and white. So many possibilities to incorporate into a cross-disciplinary thesis."

"I see. Um, what if the crow was white?" Maddie asked.

"White crow?"

"Yes."

"No such thing."

She slipped the folder of student assignments into her briefcase and teased, "Communications and crows, you say?"

"Yes."

She smiled at Cze. "You've done it. So proud of you. It must feel so good to have that defence done."

"Yes." Cze leaned back in the chair, sighed. "Thanks, Mad, for everything."

"You're welcome."

"PhD here I come."

"Like hell. Get a real job."

"Interview next week," Cze crossed fingers. "Full-time."

"Wozniak, you're not all that." Maddie lovingly grazed Cze's hand. "But you are." She swept the clunky math manipulatives off the coffee table and into her oversized purse.

"Nerd," said Cze.

"It takes one —" She called up to the second floor, "Okay, bud! Done brushing your teeth? Let's go!"

"Comin'." Decker Wozniak came bounding down the stairs, backpack in tow, his wavy mahogany locks falling out from beneath his red toque. Eyes pierced from behind his glasses. The boy had his father's strange and beautiful eyes and his mother's myopia.

"Got your helmet? Hockey PE today," Cze reminded him.

"I suck at hockey. Smallest in class. Always last one picked. Slow to get in a rhubarb. Glasses always slide down my face. Then I get blindsided."

"Get your boots on. Gloves, too," Maddie said. "You're still in Peewee Division. Don't worry about rhubarbs and blindsides."

Cze tugged Decker's toque over ears. "You'll catch on. Let's go out to the lake this weekend."

"Is it safe?" Maddie wondered aloud, remembering when the Nelson boy fell through that one year.

"We've been in a deep freeze for the last two months. You'd be hard-pressed to get through with an auger," Cze assured her.

Maddie pulled out her car keys, hefted her bag onto her shoulder, grabbed her cell phone from the entry table. "C'mon, bud."

"Come to the lake with Deck and me this weekend. Full moon. Skate. You could count and divide the stars in the sky and whisper equations to me."

"Weirdo." Maddie smiled and bent to kiss Cze on the lips. "Teacher party this weekend."

"Oh?"

"Forgot?"

"Yes."

"Teacher party."

"Oxymoronic?"

"Watch the drinking today, okay?" She opened the door for Decker. "I'm so proud of you, Wozniak. Love you so much."

Blizzard cold. Snow blew.

Maddie pulled the door shut.

He eased the dimmer switch to low. In his semi-haze went through the shelves on the mirrored cabinet in search of his meds. He twisted the cap and tipped the pill bottle labelled Vicodin into the palm of his hand. Dusty remnants. Empty. "Fuck, fuck." He desperately licked the powder and crumbs. A bit of a hit, but nowhere near enough. Cze closed the cabinet and stared at his reflection. Just to be certain he stuck out his tongue. Mirrored: check. He smiled. Mirrored: check. He gave the finger. Mirrored: check. How did he become this hairy derelict fuckup with those strange pale-blue eyes? An electrifying jolt of the migraine pierced behind his right ear, seemingly through his brain, striking at the back of his left eyeball. "Fucking ow." He hit the side of his head with his right hand. The jolt subsided. The smell of camphor mixed with that of the maple bacon drifting up from the kitchen. He padded over the decorative red Persian runner that his mother had purchased uncharacteristically on impulse from a travelling caravan. He slowly pushed open the door at the end of the runner, the end of the hallway. The boy was a small lump in the bed. The boy had also been suffering through some virus over the last week. Unlike his father, the child was taking it well — in stride. Cze navigated quietly around the wheelchair, leaned toward the boy, and listened carefully — he could hear the congestion. He laid his hand over the boy's forehead and felt fever. Cze studied his son and considered again his misfortune. He wasn't a very good parent and obviously she was no better. He gently pulled the covers around his son. In addition to the chills from the sickness, there were drafts in the old house this August morn. While slowly making his way out of the bedroom he saw the laces of running shoes ribbon from beneath the dresser, and mourning washed over him. He reminded himself: throw out the old footwear. He carried on and stumbled upon a scatter of Lego building blocks. Pain drove up his body from the soles of his feet. "FU—" Cze clamped his mouth. The boy continued to sleep. "—ck me," Cze whispered. As he closed the door to his son's bedroom, he wished that his world would taper to simplicity.

It was entirely appropriate, considering the circumstances.

2

割り当て

assignment: *wariate*

He had been waiting. The second time in four months that Cze had met with him. This time, a special assignment.

The PUBLISHER.

The gold nameplate read *The PUBLISHER*. Consider the simplicity of *the*. Capitalize it alongside the uppercase letters of *PUBLISHER* with the conservative application of Times New Roman. Clearly *PUBLISHER* is grand in comparison. Words have power. The printed word has power. Trouillot and Anderson knew it. Milocz knew it. Cze sat in the reception area with aching head in hands and eyes considering the *The*. Christ, he thought, his compulsive nature and fascination for semantics might be the death of him. Mr. Wozniak, *The PUBLISHER* will see you now. Would she say it like that? he wondered. Or perhaps, *The PUBLISHER* is now ready for you, Mr. Wozniak. Or maybe she would announce, His Royal Highness, My Lord *The PUB* —

"He's ready to see you."

Mack Smith was the publisher of the *Ezra Herald* which was an affiliate of the reformed Johnson & Smith Group (J&SG). The giant of a man settled behind the desk, tented his fingertips, and displayed an excessive set of perfectly white oversized teeth. When the customary greeting was done, he closed his mouth. Strangely, Cze considered applause. Smith, now in his late seventies, had made a considerable fortune with the sale of his regional television, radio, and newspaper assets to global corporation Johnson Communications. As part of the deal, the board of directors agreed to leave Smith in a figurehead position at the stepping-stone *Ezra Herald* until his voluntary retirement. He would groom journalists in print media and give them broadcast experience at Ezra Television stationed next door. They would move up the ladder to larger markets within the corporation. Smith was essentially a silent partner who could step down (or back up) at any time. He still thrived on the business of print journalism and was enthralled by how the new technology was changing communications, allowing for cross-media opportunities and empowering the whole business of media: more power, more money. Although his time in the field was long over, Smith was skilled at scouting talent. He knew then and he knew now without doubt that Cze Wozniak was one of the most brilliant journalists he had ever seen.

Please and thank you. He had finally arrived.

3

風
wind: *kaze*

September 2018. Peculiar windstorm.

Streams of pink light fell at soft angles through the protective pines, oaks, and cottonwoods into the clearing within the sacred grove he had meticulously tended all these years. Places and spaces begin to change with age, too. A place that once nourished the soul now a place that echoed with loneliness. Suddenly a cold north wind crept in. His cane rolled away along the edge of the stone bench. A rustle spawned by random rain cold as ice. Hail imminent. I see, *sou ka.* Kousuke rose slowly and thoughtfully, then bent down to pick up the cane. A robin toddled bashfully near his hand and then flew off. A small grace: he was pleased and grateful to be able to rise up from his bend. At his age nothing was done quickly or without great effort. He secured the ball cap on his head and tilted the brim down.

Emerging from the grove, he proceeded cautiously down the slope of the hill following the path of river rocks that snaked to the modest straw-coloured home nearby. Sometimes a stray rock was gently knocked in line with the tip of his cane. The slow walk along the path was part of his daily constitutional. Less sure-footed. Growing increasingly doubtful about everything was part of the aging process and he accepted this. But at this moment the wind and rain picked up pace, and so did he. Without warning his cap was snatched by a gust. He turned to watch it cartwheel southward. No time for sentimental attachment. He continued angling forward with bald head charging. He didn't see or hear the unusual spectacle of sparrows, starlings, crows, shrikes, and nuthatches criss-crossing chaotically above him. They flew out of the protection of the woods shortly after Kousuke did. It was unusual for birds to take flight during this kind of storm, and of course they were having difficulty navigating — it was nearly impossible to recover while in mid-flight. He also did not see that behind him the birds were falling from the sky, dropping dead.

Pea-sized hail began to bounce around him; soon the hail was the size of golf balls. Hurt like hell upon impact. Short of breath and knees aching, he was glad to be under cover of the porch where he collapsed onto the bench, leaning against the house. He rubbed the small bumps that had formed atop his head. Those odd hairs sprouting on his back and now the bumps on his head — he was becoming more and more repulsive by the day.

The house was solid and held its own against the prairie blizzards, hailstorms, floods, and hurricane-force winds.

He had used wood and river stones indigenous to the area and managed to juxtapose the unusual styles of Canadian log house with Ryukyuan mythology. For example, to ward off evil spirits he had carved a pair of *shisa* lions and set them on either side of the front-porch stairs. He was a hard worker. Over time he bought the land around him as it became available. Gradually family farmhouses and fields grew up around his house. Rows of caragana, poplar, cottonwood, evergreen were strategically cultivated and pruned on the arid lands to establish some boundary between one Kana property and the other, and also served to buffer against the ever-present wind. From the air it was an amazing sight: a circular crop system of fields with tree-boundary mazing, multiple establishments all rippling out from Kousuke's original home in the centre.

As the flash hailstorm subsided, he made his way around to the back of the house. He inspected the pitted south siding, the shredded gladioli and irises, the broken branches of the lilac bushes, and then the trees. The trees on his property had grown dense in a perfect semi-circle that fortressed the structure primarily from westerly elements. It had become apparent over time that the tree trunks and arms that enveloped the greenhouse were misshapen and unruly. The growth had lost its intent, had suffered from some neglect — or rather from the decline of an aging keeper. Kousuke saw that one of the glass panels had shattered. Shards large and small had fallen on the west-side vegetables. The delicate yellow flowers of the bitter melon he had been tending, the daikon tops he had been encouraging, the *satō kibi* sugar cane he had been attempting to produce had all been showered with glass.

Kousuke pointed to the sky, cursing at and seemingly conjuring with his cane a developing corkscrew. The wild whorl dropped down from the dusty sky in front of his house. The strange twister brought a widening radius of oceanic scents that reminded Kousuke of his younger brother. He and his brother had been taken over the East China Sea by a climactic vortex, levitating for a time, and then back again where the whorl had very gently dropped Kousuke on the shore. It then took his brother back out to the ocean and drilled into the aqua depths to the legendary *nirai kanai*. Kousuke screamed for his younger brother as the tail of the wind whipped into the sea, ringing and swinging like a machete. Kousuke ran, then swam, then bobbed, and called in half-chokes to his brother. Gone.

That was ocean.

This, the prairie.

He watched from the hill as the windstorm wrangled winterkill tumbleweeds, flung random rubbish, and spiralled detritus up above the boughs of the tallest trees. This particular dirt devil was an anomaly, a freak of nature. He'd seen a lot of that over the course of his lifetime — freaks of nature. "Where are you from: *maa kara yaibiiga?*" He shook his cane at the twister. The old man's address of this other ancient unapologetic. "I know you. I know you! Have you come for me, too?"

His thought processes shuffled up and down now and then, faded in and out, here and there. But despite memory lapses, he was still sharper than most who were a fraction of his age. Strangely, while his memory, eyesight, and hearing were on the decline, his sense of smell seemed to intensify and came to compensate for the other senses. Smells carried so many strong memory triggers for Kousuke. He could smell a bit of that westbound *kuroshio* that surrounded the Ryukyuan archipelago: that black stream had travelled from the East China Sea and was here in the air. He sloshed the smells around in his head, conjuring from its dark blue depths *kombu* for *ashitibichi* soup, *katsuobushi* shavings for tofu, the most exquisite sea salt *masu*, and the memory of his brother running along the shore throwing all sorts of sea creatures back into the ocean after *kuroshio's* high-tide bounty. There is a peculiar smell after high tide. What was it doing on the Canadian prairies? Maybe the wind and water travelled through the Ryukyu *shotō* somehow before it arrived here. Nevertheless, the island scents were washing over him. There it was.

In the early 1900s Kousuke crossed the Pacific as part of the Ryukyuan labour diaspora. There was great poverty, and in small geographies one can be displaced by dominant powers only so much before flight is necessary. Further back in time, the once-flourishing island kingdom had lost their sovereignty to Japan's Satsuma warriors in 1609. Then there was the eventual annexation by Meiji Japan in 1879, accompanied by heightened efforts to assimilate, industrialize, and Westernize. A cyclical narrative as old as creation stories, mythology, and fairy tales. Then *tetsu no bofu*. The bloodiest campaign of the Second World War staged on the largest of the islands, Okinawa, where one of every four islanders died. Followed by American occupation, Indigenous land appropriation, and militarization — parasitic forevermore. In various diasporic waves many islanders migrated to places with a similar climate like Hawaii, Brazil, Peru, Argentina, and the Philippines. But in 1907 Kousuke Kana travelled from Yomitan all the way to Canada with little money and a small bag of island seeds and plant slips. After months on the ocean, the *Monteagle* docked first in San Francisco, where Kousuke saw so many different kinds of people. He soon came to realize that learning a new language was the least of his adaptation challenges — there were other things that mattered in this country, such as the colour of his skin and hair, his small stature, his facial features. The passenger ship carried on up the Pacific Northwest to Vancouver, Canada, where it met with anti-Asian race riots upon landing. He didn't settle there as many from mainland Japan did; he carried on by train through the Rocky Mountains and beyond the foothills where there was work with the railroad, coal mines, and farming. It was a place where wheat fields blanketed the land, stretching long toward what must have been the end of the earth.

For several months he simply wandered through the prairie, destitute. Acclimation proved a long and lonely process for Kousuke. Smelling his new world. Hiding. Starving.

Watching. Listening. He was a quiet boy who seemed to arouse suspicion and draw curious stares wherever he went. His eyes were large, amber, and elongated, his shoulders unusually broad. His skin was not white or black, and neither was it quite the tone of Blackfoot or Cree. A newer category of skin colour always posed a taxonomy problem — especially for immigration forms and the gradients of discriminatory practice to be doled out. Chinese. Japanese. Korean. Taiwanese. It didn't matter that he was from the Ryukyu Islands. The hemispheric subtleties, longitudinal and latitudinal increment, not a concern here. All the same colour of categorization: yellow. What is your ethnicity? Asian. But even in the Japanese-Canadian subcultural community it was known that Kousuke was from *those islands* and therefore silently, quietly, categorized all by himself in an unmentionable subaltern class. The first and the only. He was a Ryukyuan.

There was little known about his background — or about the obscure island chain he was from, for that matter — for over time, much of the provenance of his people, along with a quarter of the population, including his entire family, had died in *that* war, their histories erased. He was part of the history silenced, and silent.

Oddly, there was one thing he wished for in the beginning that would have made him feel like he belonged. He wished someone would have asked if he was hungry, asked him to sit down and share a meal. His mother said these words all the time throughout the day, afternoon, and evening: you must be hungry, boy, sit down. But no one ever said that to Kousuke in the early years in this new land. You simply cannot trust someone who is different. Never mind inviting them into your home. The dust, you know.

Admittedly, language was key in establishing relationship here and young Kousuke spoke little English. His forms of communication were comprised of the island language of *uchinaaguchi*, some Japanese, and an ability to draw. He was eager to connect and establish relationships in this place where working with the land and sky were so important. Kousuke knew the language of land and sky. He had come from a place that prayed to the land, mountains, sea, and air. A place where little things such as a speck of dirt, a wisp of wind, or a raindrop held minor gods within. He understood and respected the cycle of planting and harvest. In a region where agriculture meant everything, that knowledge could open the door of opportunity. But skin colour. Who would take the time to learn that this young man possessed such knowledge? It was a risk to let a Ryukyuan in.

It was difficult for Kousuke to find a job. Struggles and obstacles presented themselves in many ways. For so very long he was alone in developing his own theories of harvest in the prairie landscape. Reinterpreting through a Ryukyuan lens, he set about trans-frameworking numerous ideas of ocean harvest to prairie harvest. Though his personal life was drought-ridden, his ideas for enriching the land budded and stretched in novel ways and he even contemplated augmenting irrigation systems with the practice of geomancy and divination in this arid new world.

He drew out his ideas on oilcloth, discarded rice bags, even faded old newspapers — all became valuable palimpsests. Finally, he struck metaphoric gold in scavenging an old schoolhouse chalkboard and saved enough money for a box of white chalk. And the curiosities grew.

He had extraordinary perseverance in his aloneness (aloneness among people who reject or ignore you for reasons that don't make sense is the bravest kind of brave) and kept inching forward through a path dotted with myriad failures. But through failures and insecurities there was no denying that he had a gift: he possessed an innate relationship with the land that he was feeding in an unorthodox way. Over time his prairie knowledge blended harmoniously with his island knowledge, and it was all at once pragmatic and mystical. He grew critical in his own unique way to the prairie landscape and the business of agriculture. Kousuke could smell water, smell the dirt, smell the weather, and he could still smell the island in the air. Looks of contempt were replaced with understanding — one man at a time, one family at a time, one cultural articulation at a time. Kousuke, it turned out, became likeable despite his foreignness. In time he found a niche and almost miraculously became a successful prairie farmer whose land acquisitions grew exponentially and incredibly, based on merit.

But his story started in 1888: over a century ago. Yes, Kousuke Kana was, at one hundred thirty years old, the oldest man on earth.

Mm-hm, the oldest. Is that a problem?

4

木妙な雨

strange rain: *kimyōna ame*

Dead birds.

Crows, magpies, sparrows, gulls all seemed to be circling his house en masse these days. Even swarms of bees and wasps, clouds of monarchs, and abnormally large dragonflies. Creatures were simply falling to the ground. These flying and dying things were at first a wonder, but now Kousuke's reaction had turned to horror. He stepped around a lifeless sparrow and shook his cane at the birds in flight. "I've done nothing to antagonize you. Quit flying over my house. Quit dying on my land," Kousuke yelled skyward over the wind. "Go away. I repeat, go away."

Arching, he proceeded to slowly pick up the larger bits of clutter that the windstorm had left behind. Pierced a few with a branch that served also as a cane. Nearly every movement made was with reservation. There was a weariness to all of it.

At a certain point in life, death (or rest), though not fully comprehensible, seemed welcome. In fact, once he did officially die. He remembered the moment clearly. Upon arrival Kousuke said to Death: "You must be hungry, sit down." Death was inclined to indulge the old man and sat for a while. Kousuke served him stir-fried *gōya* on top of rice with some *nattō* on the side. "What is your verdict?" Kousuke queried knowing that the rice was perfectly cooked — well-cooked rice improves the flavours of everything else on the plate. Death enjoyed the aroma, texture, and flavour of the rice. It's true. Kousuke had cooked perfect rice. Then Death tried the *gōya*, and then the *nattō*. He wiped the corners of his mouth, caped himself, and disappeared.

~~~~~

s o . His back ached when he bent down. Predictably, the place behind his right ear (a farming accident) spiked with pain whenever he problem-solved beyond certain limitations. His knees suffered, too. They often wobbled and sometimes they even locked. The cartilage had long worn away on the left side, to the point where even the cortisone shots had become ineffective. Still, that didn't stop him from walking to his grandson's house just over the hill or walking to his great-granddaughter's house near the old cottonwood. Despite the pain, he enjoyed a nice walk. And the family had learned to measure his need for independence with assistance when required. He'd earned the right, after all, to do as he pleased to some degree. Living on his own surrounded by various family acreages suited him just fine. They kept the outside world away. More importantly, they insulated him from Western media — an entity that he had come to understand as fundamentally deceptive. Interviews were granted once. But he became wary when the family found out how ravenous reporters were. Interviews stopped shortly after his one hundred and tenth birthday.

JUST AS SUDDENLY as it arrived, the wild wind spun away, its volume and velocity quickly dissipated over the coulees until an innocuous puff. He proceeded down the slope to his house.

Down he eased to a crumpled McDonald's bag. Obvious trash to most, but to him the litter was rather something more — symbolized as Kadena Air Force Base. He picked up a few oddities that the wind had left behind: a wool sock that was unravelling at the heel, a laptop charger, a small leather handbag missing the shoulder strap. He stuffed the assorted garbage in a weathered plastic Safeway bag he had in his pocket. The military presence occupied nearly a fifth of the island, establishing a state of permanent installation, slowly subsuming and compromising an ancient culture. It takes at least a decade for the earth to reclaim progress for agriculture. A couple steps forward, he reached for the plastic Coca-Cola bottle that he imagined as yet another proposed American air force base, Henoko. What was the official Washington stance about Japan's recent landfill approval on Okinawa? *Japan's favourable decision helps to support the Pentagon in cementing a geographically optimal, operationally resilient, and politically sustainable posture.* Something to that effect. The Governor of Okinawa had ruled against the base. Yet the construction pushed on, appropriating land, desecrating. Just unjust. Any way you looked at it, just unjust. Environmental destruction and cultural genocide — in the case of these islands interconnected. Then there was the matter of Yonaguni and China, territorial waters. Political manipulation disrupted the earthly flow. Yet to be determined how it impacts the divine. He defiantly crushed the Coca-Cola bottle into the plastic bag. It flinched back with a crackle.

Up high, a scuttle-ruck of birds in the tree. He regretted looking upward at that moment, for he spied a ragged white grocery bag that had lodged itself in the top of the amur maple. The tree had grown tall enough now that he would need a ladder to retrieve the bag. They told him not to climb any more. Urged him to stay level. The amur maple had been planted so many years ago in memory of his wife, Emiko. First a mysterious virus. Then respiratory problems. Problems everywhere. Soon entire cities, entire countries will be quarantined. Fiction. The bag was strangling a spray of the tree, compromising its being — leaves and branches asphyxiated. "*Sa,*" he sighed. He couldn't wait. Kousuke believed that the tree held Emiko's *kami.* "I'm climbing." Besides, if they didn't die trying, old people were forgiven their petulance or old belief systems.

It wouldn't do, he thought. He went to the shed to retrieve the ladder.

For a moment he was besieged with memories of her. So thick was the onslaught that it verged on smothering, and once again he tipped his head upward and gulped for an air pocket. Branched thoughts of her and the house, her and the children, her and the garden, her and the indecipherable words and tangled translations that emerged from her throat. The memories suddenly seemed to consume him from the inside out. The pain from his back radiated, doubling him over. There was a horrifying cracking sound of bones that resounded from within the weave of his shoulders. He quieted. Pain eased.

As he climbed the tree, sparrows sprayed but the crows stubbornly stayed put, flitting and hopping, then plotting in the higher branches. A sub-flock of sparrows quickly reconvened on the nearby clothesline and hammocked silently as though a panel of discriminating judges. They cawed and chipped at him. In the face of their protests, Kousuke batted at the bag with his cane and missed. He tried a second time and successfully hooked the bag. It smelled like pond ice up in the trees. He slowly descended, folded the ladder, and proceeded back to the shed. A crow landed lightly on the tip of the ladder. Kousuke was curious about the bird's uncharacteristic behaviour. Pain shot up his right side beneath the rib cage. He jerked and the bird flew away. He laid the ladder down, rested a bit, then switched, hoisting it with his left arm. He tried to dismiss the pain.

There was an enormous amount of effort now required for him to be mobile. Yes, it had come to this. Consideration of the ability to move determined his day-to-day living. There was also the matter of placating his addled brain. He just didn't know how much longer he could hold on before death. Prolonging life seemed such an inefficient use of time. Overexerted, he sat on the porch step for a while minding that one nail on the first step that needed a bit of banging. Saunder said he'd do it. He was getting paid by the estate to keep his yard. But the man was by Kousuke's account lazy and had a habit of making unfulfilled promises. He thought his twenty-five-year-old great-great-great-granddaughter — his favourite, Anya — could have done better. She seemed to carry her unambitious husband. There was a small concern about this relationship — even though she was a headstrong and pragmatic woman, he thought Saunder was abusing Anya. But no one sensed this but Kousuke. It stung to think about it, so he always ignored this little thing when it came to mind — though it arose constantly. Kousuke absently clutched and unclutched the handle of his cane.

There was an odd ambient stillness. He could hear his own breathing. Unnatural quietude. Kousuke sniffed. He smelled something chemical — more specific, metallic. His heart began to race.

Kousuke knew the smell of death. Suddenly birds began dropping from the sky and landing with soft thuds. The sound of a bird hitting the ground was deceivingly benign. The sight of many of them falling askew was horrific.

He rose from the porch as fast as he could, but with that movement came a terrible pain, as though something was clawing at his right shoulder blade from within. Thud. Thud. A downpour of birds. They were falling faster. Raining birds. He stopped, hands on his knees, allowing the rest of his body to catch up to the quick movement. His breathing became progressively laboured. Kousuke tapped the pain at his right knee with his fist, almost attacking the meridian, trying to distract the climbing pain. The torment clawed up to just behind his right shoulder and rippled outward. "Stop. Ahh. Stop," he moaned in anguish. Then, something within him exploded. More birds fell. Thud. Kousuke sank to his knees, retching.

This was not a quiet time.

5

まだ

not quite yet: *mada*

"IT'S TIME," she wrote with the black Sharpie. There was a rasp in her chest as she struggled to breathe. "GOING."

"Maddie. Things will turn around. The doctors —" He became increasingly agitated.

"CAN'T," she scribbled.

The events played out in Cze's mind.

Over and over.

A nightmare.

Decker attended the school Maddie taught at, Ezra Elementary. The commute couldn't be more perfect. Highway 3 was usually busy as a rule. In addition, there was some blowing snow. So, on this day Maddie decided to take the quieter secondary road. They approached the Ridge Road intersection at the same time as the van. A new, larger stop sign had recently been installed. Visibility was low with a bit of whiteout and perhaps some black ice — whatever the reason, the van went through the stop. The driver's side, Maddie's side, was directly impacted. The vehicle flipped mid-air and rolled several times on the ground before coming to an overturned stop in the ditch. Papers, texts, math manipulatives, and hockey equipment strewn on the road, in the snow. Debris was found a few miles east on the Monarch Hutterite Colony.

She lay in the hospital bed. The collision had shattered her. This was no longer a whole healthy body. Rather, it was broken down into component parts, each requiring a different kind of medical attention from all sorts of specialists. Her face was wrapped in bandages. Tubes transported fluids, crossing and webbing her body like a game of Cat's Cradle.

"DECK," she wrote.

Cze knew she was giving up. "Decker needs you. I need you. Don't you fucking leave us, Maddie. D-don't."

Gently grazed her hand with his fingertips. He held the pen in her hand. "Write. Try."

She dragged the pencil across the page. "WRITE." Her exposed eye glimmered hazel-soft against the layers of bandages. Long brown lashes clumped with tears.

"Stay, Maddie."

She shuddered. "TRY."

The night first took his clarity and then it broke something inside. It happened so quickly there was no time for confession. Storm filled with rumble. Sky lit with crackle. Lightning veined and laced so delicately, so bright, piercing the blackness exposing the identifiable Ezra. The skyline, Coal Mine No. 5, the Barrie Mill, the High Level Bridge. A stray stream of light bolted through the window of the hospital room seeking her body. It banked off the east wall, leaving an isolated scorch, then angled over to the north wall, leaving another burnt umber marking, and deflected into Maddie's left foot. The current swam through her. Cze remembered screaming. "Mad! Mad!" The smell of burnt hair filled the room. He carefully touched the top of her head. Exit wound.

And then a miracle.

Maddie Wozniak uttered her first word since the car accident. "Cze?"

But it is here. Here is where. It is here. Where bit by bit the narrative unsharpened for Cze, became scribbled and graffitied, and began to hurt mostly in his head. The turning point is here with Maddie's miraculous recovery. He'd been by her side through those first steps — steps back, then steps forward. Then steps away.

WHY? Cze couldn't understand. What had happened?

Over time the recovered Maddie was not the same woman he had known. After the remarkable healing she bizarrely turned into a woman possessed. She proceeded to empty accounts, take everything the couple had worked for, then vanished, leaving him with a broken boy.

⟨⟨⟨

CZE MANAGED HIS WAY DOWN the isolated prairie side road. The rocks spit beneath the worn tires of the rental. He wasn't accustomed to driving on gravel, a task made especially difficult in a small compact with ineffectual tires. Every now and then he'd fishtail near the ditch, taking out overgrown roadside foliage — thatches of thistle and fox-tail. After the urge became unbearable, he pulled off on a side road near a malformed tree. Desperately went for his cigarettes, fished for his lighter. Addiction. As soon as the cigarette was between his lips, nerves calmed. He pulled out his cell phone.

"He's going to resist that. Don't introduce anything new while I'm gone. Keep everything the same as what he is used to, Mom. Keep his routines. Keep his patterns." Cze inhaled deeply and exhaled the smoke. "Yes, after this trip I intend on quitting. Don't forget to plug the fountain in his room before he goes to bed. The babble of the water soothes him. Only use the red-and-black plaid flannel comforter to cover him at night. There are three of them in the linen closet and the one on his bed. You can't go wrong there. Remember to use those brown paper bags for his lunch, folded down three times. Check the motor on the wheelchair every day. Physio Saturday mornings. I ordered a Lego kit for him online. Did it arrive?" Cze tapped out another cigarette. "Oh, good. Yes, I know this is the first time I've been away from him. Never for a week." He tried to wind the conversation down. "Yes. I understand, Mom. I intend on stopping. Soon. No, I don't want to orphan him. Okay. I'll call you later. Yes. Gotta go." Cze hung up before she could respond.

He thought about Maddie. Sank to his haunches and hung his head. Picked up a stick and drew the symbol for *pi* in the dirt. "Miss you, fuck you," he said to the dirt and the question circled his mind for the millionth time: *Where the fuck are you?* He took a deep breath, regained composure. Pressed his cigarette into the ground.

<hr>

IT WAS A BEAUTIFUL DAY for a scouting trip. Scoping out the prairie landscape seemed a sensible thing to do upon arrival. Despite his frayed nerves, he appreciated the day. This part of the country was serene and had a way of soothing. The feathered clouds spread-eagled before him. A speckle of farmhouses in the distance. In a split-second Cze again caught himself losing control atop the gravel, recovered, and slowed. Renting an off-road vehicle would have been more appropriate. Obviously.

He caught sight of his dust trail in the rear-view mirror. Then he caught a rut in the gravel. Ahead, a combine tractor rose from a dip in the road and shimmered in the heat. He was losing control. He over-adjusted allowing for the tractor to pass. But the slope of the road and the loose gravel — he couldn't hold the line. "Sh-shit. Deck. I'm sorry, Decker." The word *orphan*. Essentially it meant that both parents were gone. But there was still Maddie. Wasn't there? A recessed memory seemed to be surfacing. There was still Mad — He suddenly found himself airborne.

6

前兆

this is strange: *zenchō*

The pain abated after time. But there was a remnant. *Toge da sagashite.* He plucked a peculiar splinter lodged in his right shoulder that seemed to have emerged from within. He examined it and was immediately disgusted. The splinter looked like a ragged feather. This was it. He was on course for death — a weird and perhaps vulgar death. He tossed the splinter into the rose-bush. Hopefully death would be quick. He rubbed his right shoulder with his left hand. Still hurt. Took a deep breath. He sat for a while on the top step and simply tracked the delicate stratocumulus scroll. It unfolded like the prelude to a great *eisa* composition. He could get lost in the sky, always could. "Yes, yes, I remember. In a moment. *Sa.*" He rose to his feet and pulled the garden gloves from his pockets.

Treading lightly, he began to gently pick up the birds. He couldn't manage the complex footwork and after three birds, he decided to leave them for Saunder to pick up.

THE INSTRUMENT HAD BEEN sealed after Emiko died. He set it down on the Formica table. Emptied his pockets of his hanky (his left eye was constantly weeping), a couple of cellophaned hard candies, and a wristwatch. He then took care to wash his hands and fingers thoroughly. Compelled to wash over and over again. Wash the day off.

Glimpsed the mirror. Unexpected angle. Ghost? No, a version of himself. His physicality was changing so quickly in recent years, even his own reflection was taking him by surprise. A once-black thicket of hair had become so translucent white and thin that in a certain light he could see his entire scalp through the sparse crop of filaments. In fact, he thought, there was less hair and more exposed skin now. Furthermore, upon rigorous study, his scalp seemed to be balding in large patches — all around. He held his hands to the light. Webbed. Even his skin was becoming transparent. "You're dust," he said to his reflection. "Dust."

He saw movement behind him in the mirror. The box on the table shuddered ever so slightly.

It was still moving when he transported it to the couch. Nothing much surprised him anymore, not at this age. He pushed the matching ottoman from the armchair closer to the couch, and then perched before the box. Apprehension. Discomfort.

It had become unseasonably hot. The global weather was reporting bedlam — hurricanes, typhoons, blizzards where snow had never been seen, flooding where there had historically been desert. Anyways. He delicately thumbed the top button of his favourite tan cardigan, found its edge. As he commenced down the row, button by button, he discovered a hole. This would not do. Another washing, he thought, and it would undoubtedly unravel and become irreparable. The thing in the box thudded. A weave of thread should do the trick — that is, if his fingers would allow. But the work could wait until later, under the flare of lamp and magnifying glass. Gently, he laid the garment on the chafed arm of the couch carefully picked off a fragment of lint. He adjusted his short-sleeved cotton shirt — this too, worn to diaphanous.

The packaging tape was thick and secure, difficult to strip. He was sensitive to the finely sifted attic dust floating about and began sneezing. Even the sneezing rattled his body. He had to brace for each one. Suddenly mid-sneeze he heard the skid on gravel. A car likely compromising its suspension over the lip of the ditch — sounds of brakes screeching, tempered glass giving, metal crushing and bending. He'd come to understand rural sounds — the sound of a car lopping into the ditch, for example, had an alarming symphony.

"Should I go? I better not."

7

不時着

crash landing: *fujichaku*

Something happened.

Cze sat in the car for a while, watched the tractor's dust cloud disappear over the hill. The driver of the tractor hadn't even noticed. Spun out so fast he felt like he was on a high. Afraid to move. After some time, he unbuckled, uncoiled, and crabbed his way through the wheat field away from the wreckage. He lay in a fetal position, comforted somewhat in the isolation of the stalks. Then he reset the Boston Bruins cap on his head, proceeded to touch his face, scratch his stubble, test the movement of his body parts. From what he could ascertain from his horizontal position, he had a mild headache, no broken bones. Sky was blue. Check. Ten fingers on his hands. Check. He began suturing the air, watching his wrist and fingers manage. "Yup, they work." He stared at the back of his hand.

The roll had put a substantial dent in the roof. The hood was bent out of shape. It took a bit of struggle, but he managed to get the trunk open. Scrambled contents tumbled out into the long golden stalks. The Nikon camera bag, his knapsack, his laptop. That's all he was concerned about. He took a spot beneath the lone cottonwood, pulled off his cap. Looked up to the sky, let the wind cool his face. Ran his hands nervously through his thick mess of cola-coloured hair, put his ball cap back on. Blood streamed from above his right brow. He lay back and began to fall into sleep.

"You okay? You okay, boy?"

Cze looked up from where he was lying on the grass. The silhouette moved about until the sun shone on his face. Cze saw an old mountain cloaked as a human being.

"I'm fine."

8

チャンス
chance: *chansu*

"You should see a doctor. Whiplash. Concussion. You'll have that scar above your eye for the rest of your life. It needs stitchin'. This bandage won't do. You've got a nice face beneath that stubble —" Kousuke half waved, referencing Cze's scruff. "Shame now. Ugly."

"No, there's no need."

It was a good opportunity for Cze to take in the old man close up — about five foot nothing, with glittery eyes that almost blazed out from a sun-dried face, and something that Cze surprisingly sensed, a strange voltage emanating from his fingers.

"No, no. I'm fine. Thanks for bandaging me up." He carefully placed his cap on his head and looked around the modest room — manageable for an old man. It smelled of fresh bread. A few ball caps and plaid coats on wall hooks above a thick wooden bench, some kind of long box, maybe for an instrument of some sort, he couldn't quite place it.

The house was sparse and spotless except for various tidy stacks of books — an incredible collection. Derrida, Foucault, and Fanon here; Spivak, Bhabha, and Chatterjee there; Yamanokuchi, Medoruma, and Iha Fuyu in another; and a stack that intrigued Cze particularly composed of Tolstoy, Chekhov, and Dostoevsky. It is possible that this old Asian man could have read all of these? Cze then caught sight of the array of sticky notes tacked to the cupboards and the fridge:

STOVE OFF
DR. SENADA TUES 9am
8 PILLS DAILY
NHK, SUN 7pm
LOCK DOORS
BREAD
AVOID PROCESSED MEATS
249 CHILDREN
JIUSHI IN FRIDGE
DON'T EVER TALK TO STRANGERS

The daylight seemed to fill the space with melancholy. He settled on the view from the window. The dark clouds rolled in over the yellow wheat fields, and the wind rhythmically blew about the tufts of the dead birds.

"You should hire an apocalypse expert," Cze said, tapping at the edge of the bandage above his eye. "I'm half expecting Tippi Hedren to run in through your f-front door."

For a moment, Cze had an urge to contact Smith. Mysterious bird deaths would certainly be a story for the newspaper. He needed to refocus. Nothing trumped a feature story about the oldest man in the world saving a reporter.

Kousuke smiled and poured the tea. "I think they're getting some conservationist or biology professor from the university to come by. They'll take care of it."

"They?"

"Family." Kousuke stared at the Kagoshima tea leaves swishing at the bottom of his cup. "I'm surrounded by them. Protected by them. Mostly they want to keep the 'scourge of humanity' away." Kousuke arched his eye and laughed. "Their euphemism for the media."

Cze rose from the chair.

"Sit down. Green tea will be good for you. Tow truck on its way."

"What will they do if they find out a stranger is on the land, in your house?"

"Kick your butt clear to the Trans-Canada eastbound. Whatever they do, it will be unceremonious. They tie the knots pretty tight around me. I'll also be reprimanded."

"Why did you?" Cze unslung his knapsack onto the floor. His sketchbook fell open at Kousuke's feet. He reached for it.

"Well, under the circumstances, you needed immediate help. But I think I was mostly influenced by the cap." Kousuke winked.

"My lucky Boston Bruins hat."

"Bobby Orr. A legend in my books."

"Mine, too."

"Not so lucky today."

"Nope."

"Looks like you're an artist. May I?" Kousuke retrieved the sketchbook and examined the thumbnails of crow drawings. "Hm, not bad," he said closing the book and handing it to Cze.

Cze was used to compliments on his art. His drawings had somehow held the power of fascination. It was in part how he had attracted Maddie into his life. He scribbled and doodled elaborately beside her in class. As with Kousuke, the drawings initiated questions. But now he hated Maddie.

Kousuke was old. He spoke his mind. "Don't be flattered. They're not bad. But they're not all that good, either. They lack sincerity."

"Well. Mostly I'm a wr-writer." Cze immediately stopped talking, afraid his stutter would betray him — his stutter a polygraph test of sorts. Writer. He feared there was now suspicion circling him. He didn't want to scare Kousuke away or give away any clues to his being a new member of the *scourge of humanity*.

Kousuke sensed Cze's sudden restlessness. He pressed the large sticky note affixed to the red table — scrawled in pen was BEFORE YOU LEAVE THE HOUSE. "Writer, huh? Well, I won't hold that against you." He read the first item on the list, STOVE OFF, and glanced at the stove just to be certain. He returned his gaze to Cze. "You like drawing crows?"

Cze nodded. "Crows are — well, they're good subjects to draw. And uh, they're smart, good communicators."

Kousuke looked out the window at the dead birds. "Well, not so smart — it turns out they can dive to death for no reason." He moved away from the window. "Crows are a sign of bad luck where I come from."

Suddenly a shooting pain ricocheted like a pinball between Kousuke's shoulder blades. He reached for the top of his left shoulder. His back arched then pitched forward as the pain battered a path up his spinal column and tightened between his shoulder blades. Tighter. He tried to bear the round of pain by training his sights on a crystal doorknob. Tighter. He gripped the edge of the table and focussed so hard on the facets that he imagined travelling right into the knob's core. He breathed heavily. There was a rasp.

Cze froze and watched for movement from the rigid old man. His face seemed to have drained of blood, was as grey as a clay pot. "Are you alright?" He rose from the chair. "Mr. Kana?" Cze caught the old man as he teetered. "What is it?"

"It's nothing. In the grips of being an old man, is all. However, maybe you should go."

"Yeah. The tow truck company texted that their driver was a couple minutes away from the junction. By the time I walk out there to the road, he'll be — I've kept you. Sorry." He grabbed his gear. "You sure you're okay?"

Kousuke managed a smile. "Seems we've both had challenge today."

Kousuke left his clothes in a messy pile on the floor at the foot of his bed. He walked to the full-length mirror with fear and trepidation. He turned to his side and began to breathe heavily. His reflection revealed a sight both alluring and repelling: glorious white tufts of feathers had emerged from between his shoulder blades. Blood dripped slowly from his right ear.

9

ジャックポット

jackpot: *jakkupotto*

His cell rang as soon as he entered the hotel room.

"How's he doing?" Cze kicked off his shoes. "Let me talk to him. Yes, I know he's not in a talkative mood. Nothing new. Mom, just let me talk to him."

The boy was breathing over the phone.

"Deck? There are a lot of rocks here. There's a river called the Old Man. Isn't that a funny name for a river?" Cze leaned against the wall behind the door and slid down to a crouch. "The Old Man's got a lot of rocks for your collection. I'll find some good ones."

"Okay."

"Did you start the Falcon? Over a thousand bricks. That's a challenge."

Nothing.

"Deck, I love you. I miss you."

Silence.

"Hi, Mom. He's okay, then? Is he? Good. No, I don't want

to meet Mrs. Hankinson's daughter, Sylvia. Erratic schedule, uh huh. Yes, I know he needs a mother. I'm not adopting a tone, Mom. Look, I've got another call. I'll talk to you later." Cze slid up the wall and took a deep breath before answering the call on hold. It seemed he had to don some sort of armour to mitigate the dispiriting.

"Jesus, what took you?"

"Talkin' to my mom and then had to get my wireless on."

"Your mom?"

"Yeah."

"How was the trip?"

"Well, it couldn't have been worse, and then couldn't have turned out better." As if jolted into another's skin, Cze shifted his world and unloaded his gear at the foot of the bed. He tapped at the cut above his eye. "Long story short. I totalled the vehicle without injury. Incredibly — you won't believe this — I ended up in the Kana wheat field. The old man came to my rescue."

"Holy shit." Smith was laughing. "Jackpot. So he's not completely withdrawn from society. What was he like?"

"Yeah. Uh. He's old. Wise. Looks like an old mountain or ancient oak, maybe a combination. Bandaged me up. I guess if anyone could be categorized as your typical shaman, he could." Cze laughed and fell back on the bed exhausted.

"Family running interference?"

"It was a rare situation. Right timing. Plus, he seemed to like me. So there was no family. I think they're probably onto it now, though. As I was leaving, it seemed family were drifting from different directions to the old man's place. There was a strange bird thing that happened."

"Bird thing?"

"Yeah, hundreds of birds fell from the sky on his front lawn. The family had contacted some scientists from the university. So there will be a bit of a commotion over there."

"Hm. Interesting. That *bird thing's* happening in the U.K., too." Smith contemplated a story, but the thought was fleeting. "We got a bigger story. Exclusive. What's the plan?"

"I left my sketchbook at his place. He knows I'm here. Expecting a call."

"What? You think *he's* gonna call you? That's your plan? You may have blown it. Should've interviewed him while you had the opportunity."

"Well, no photo op yet. I think I can get an exclusive if I wait." Cze tapped out a cigarette and wandered out to the balcony. He scanned the horizon. "Goddamn. It's beautiful out here."

"Call him. Tell him you'll go to his place and pick up the sketchbook."

"No, he might become suspicious and send one of his family to deliver it here. That's not what I want. I'm going to wait."

"The longer you wait, the less chance you have of getting closer. I'd advise you to start stirring."

"I'm gonna wait, and uh, there was something else." Cze lit the cigarette and took a deep breath. The smoke felt good.

"What do you mean? What else?"

"Not quite sure. But I can tell you with absolute certainty, there was something else happening with that old man. Something unusual." Cze pulled the bottle from his knapsack and set it on the nightstand.

"And being a hundred and thirty years old isn't unusual?"

Cze inhaled to full and slowly exhaled. He hadn't realized how frayed his nerves were until then.

10

楽器

instrument: *gakki*

To protect from damage it was packed with balled-up pages of the *Ryukyu Shimpo* newspaper. It had been a long time since he'd played the strings. He felt his chest pound with excitement, and then some dullish discomfort in the shoulder blades. Nausea. He stopped for a moment to catch his breath. In his periphery, he glimpsed a spider scuttle across the floor. Sensing it had been spotted, the black splatter stopped abruptly, as if believing it could become invisible if dead still. The old man kept his sights on it and retrieved a glass jar from the collection in the bottom cupboard. He circled and quickly as he could trapped the spider in the jar. When it crawled up into the jar, he covered the mason mouth with his hand, took it outside, and gently tapped the spider out of the jar into the garden over his collection of round rocks.

The overcast glowered down upon the southern Alberta farmland. Still arched with jar in hand, Kousuke looked at the advance of deepening clouds with suspicion. Tempest loomed. It was as though a story were about to begin, he thought. Then he thought that was a ridiculous thought and wanted to unthink it. But thoughts are not easily retractable. He proceeded to straighten with the help of the porch railing, moved slowly up the steps, could see the dust rise in small puffs from between the slats, and he thought about mini-pulpits.

He sat at the couch for some time, letting fatigue pass. Soon he felt the warm ooze run down his back. He braced for the growth of more feathers and another wave of pain.

11

飛行前
pre-flight: *hikō mae*

It felt like an unimaginable massacre.

Feathers were everywhere.

Someone was in for busy work.

"Several possibilities," said one of the men from the university. He crouched and picked up a bird with his gloved hands.

"These mass animal deaths can sometimes be mysterious, but are generally explainable," said scientist number two. "One possibility is shifting migration routes. Storm. Perhaps a butterfly effect. Environmental changes happening today or that happened in the past. They can ripple into unrelated problems down the line."

Some of the Kana family had gathered outside Kousuke's house with the scientists. They were hanging on every word.

"We ought to establish a cause and effect if possible." Scientist number one was prodding at a sparrow. "Any loud noises in the area before they fell?"

"Not that I'm aware of," said Saunder, whose house was closest to Kousuke's. "I'll be damned." He turned away from the group and kicked at a dead bird. Then he kicked at another and then stomped on the head of another. Only Kousuke noticed.

"Have any fallen in the fields?" queried Claire Kana. At sixty-three years old, Kousuke's daughter's daughter had never married. Kousuke thought he could smell a cancer within her — stomach region. She lived on the north end of the land, on the cusp of what was called the *durum* section. She farmed better than any of them and was currently researching seeding dates and their impact on crop qualities. She was an authority on semolina flour and was even contemplating partnering in a pasta processing plant.

"Perhaps a hoax." John Delano Charlevoix's baritone voice was distinct. J.D., as they all called him, was the tall, broad husband of Kousuke's great-grandchild, Rose. J.D. had quit the pipe over a decade ago after Rose's relentless nagging. But Kousuke knew, beneath the mask of mint-flavoured mouthwash, that J.D.'s fondness for cherry tobacco had never ceased — its presence still charmed him.

Rose, who was an authority over J.D., responded. "A hoax? That's the most ridiculous thing I've ever heard." She slowly sauntered away from the group, as usual, her jean seams making that rubbing sound at the inner thigh when she walked. There was a narcotic quality about the predictable rhythm that always had Kousuke searching for a place to nod off. That *tch-tch* sedation.

"I'm leaning toward the environmental theory. The birds' migratory patterns are askew." Emily McClung was the youngest child of Kousuke's youngest son, Heath. Kousuke's great-granddaughter. Emily was affable and at the same time annoying; she possessed large saucer eyes, pale skin with dark red hair. A vegetarian that, Kousuke knew, secretly binged unhindered on teriyaki beef jerky on Saturday nights. How did he know? He knew. Emily crouched down. "Strangely, the birds are diverse. There's an owl here and a brambling over there. Outside migratory dates. It's almost like they convened because their commonality wasn't necessarily *species*, but that they are feathered."

"Look closer, there are insects, too," said Anya. "Maybe the common thread is more fundamental. They have wings."

One of the scientists looked at the sky. "Was there anything out of the ordinary before the birds fell?"

"I'm working on this part of the land nearly every day. I can't say there was anything that would have signalled this." Saunder waved his large hands at the blanket of dead birds. "Can they contaminate us? Can you get a team in to clean this up? It's unsightly for *ojīsan*." Saunder's public concern deceived all. Kousuke cringed when the word *ojīsan* came from the man's mouth.

Everyone was talking simultaneously. The children were making a game of running between the dead birds. Frances Dement, the eldest granddaughter of Kousuke's middle son of the same name, would not have allowed the children anywhere near the scene in fear that it may be riddled with disease.

"So, nothing out of the ordinary." The one scientist was scribbling while the other was advising to keep away from the birds.

"There was a strange wind," Kousuke said. "It was like a tornado. I saw that kind of tornado once in Okinawa. It foreshadowed the one that took my brother —" They didn't even hear the old man. "A wild wind."

He was used to being lonely amid the flurry of Kana activity. The family was so loud as a group. They were like an ocean. Deafening. Habituated to cacophony and a kind of herd mentality. The way his brain was working these days, he was reminded of the time he'd fallen into that well. Was it related? Maybe not. It happened a long time ago and maybe some of the story had become skewed. But it was his first job in Canada on the west coast of British Columbia.

There was an old well near the site. Some of the workers who didn't care for the colour of his skin had thrown him in. The supervisor, Hugh Compton, finally found Kousuke and called down in the hole, asking what exactly he was doing down there. Sitting, Kousuke had told Compton. Just sitting. Kousuke remembered the echo of his words scuttled up the rocks, desperately escaping the dark. Then Compton got a few of the workers to toss down a coil. They pulled him up. He slumped motionless near the crumbling well wall where nettles and dandelion circled. What were you doin' down there, Kousuke? Kousuke told Compton he'd fallen. One of the men who'd helped him up was also one of the men who had pushed him in.

"This won't be tolerated." Compton stared his crew down. "Do you understand?"

But Kousuke had learned that in this complex new world, lockstepped with the metafictions of great faiths and aphorisms such as "all are equal in the eyes of God and leaders of men," was façade. An important lesson (in survival). And in forgiveness. It was the only way.

The setting sun shaped silhouettes of the workers as they shrugged their shoulders and walked off. The man who had pushed Kousuke in the well earlier looked over his shoulder at him and then joined back in the group conversation. They were loud; they laughed. The herd diminished into the shimmering infinity.

"*Ojīsan?*" Anya woke him from what seemed a trance. He saw her between ocean waves — it was like the sea had parted to stillness. Anya Olson Ferguson was a mix of Swedish, Irish, and Okinawan and she was the most beautiful of all the women in his family. She had fallen out of him by mistake. She was sapphiric. Beauty like this is happenstance — no god or gods could know this recipe. She was sharp as a tack at times, yet there was a gentle underpinning that always made her approachable. All things were set aside when Anya looked at him with her mischievous smile, sparkling hazel eyes.

He remembered how she loved birds once. There was a sparrow she had buried somewhere in his flower garden.

He wondered how she felt about all these dead birds. *"Hai. Dōshita no, Peck?"*

"Are you cold these days?"

"Uh, why do you ask?"

"Do you need to wear those oversized clothes? They're so baggy."

Kousuke shrugged. "Yes. Yes, I do need to wear these clothes." He waved for her to draw nearer. "This layer is to protect from the burn of summer," Kousuke teased as he fingered the light cotton shirt.

"Oh, of course, *ojīsan*. Makes absolute sense," she smiled.

"This second shirt I've had for over fifty years and has become so thin, it doesn't even count as garment." They both laughed. "And this —"

As she got closer, he saw the bruise. She'd styled her hair to conceal the right side of her face. Kousuke moved her hair aside, gently touched her face. Beneath the floral scent, the smell of some sad clay rose through Kousuke's nose and down his throat. Kousuke looked directly into Anya's sad eyes.

"I suppose one should be more careful with that retractable door. I ran straight into it with my face," she said.

"Of course. Perhaps it's time to get rid of that retractable door," Kousuke replied.

"Yes. Get rid of it."

"I hope you will. Dispense with it, and soon. Otherwise I will worry about your undue stress from that damn retractable door." Kousuke reached out to her. Held her hand. "Anya." He looked into her eyes again. "Get rid of it."

Anya smiled weakly and changed the subject.

"I'll bring you lunch in a while. It's your favourite," she said. "Chicken stew with dumplings." She suddenly realized the irony and laughed. "Because you can't get enough bird on a day like today, *ojīsan.*"

He laughed, too. "Mm, chicken stew. Ha. Looking forward to it. *Jyā mata.*" He turned, lifted his hand goodbye, and wandered back toward the house.

THE PACKING TAPE was fixed so securely to the box. An impossible task to rip off, it seemed. Crooked finger roots. He went to the kitchen. Pulled open the top drawer to the right of the fridge. Everything was in place. The telephone and address books were stacked neatly, the box of writing utensils squared to the back left of the drawer, the note paper arranged in the back right of the drawer, and the old barber scissors that were always sharp folded at the front of the drawer. When his eyes fell on the scissors, they shuddered slightly — just a slight vibration, almost imperceptible. But vibrations matter. Then he heard a soft scuttle as they opened a little, similar to the teasing spread of an origami crane just before the final score. Startled, he quickly shut the drawer, took a half-step away, and stared unblinking for a long time. He thought about the wings he was growing and decided there surely could be no phenomenon that could top that.

He was reminded that he was nothing.

That settled him down a little.

12

レゴから羽まで

from Lego to feathers: *lego kara hane made*

He knew nothing about concussions. Something about a swollen brain.

Cze vigorously rubbed his wet hair with the towel. "How's school been?" Camera pointed to the floor. He mostly saw the boy's hands and the Lego scattered about. He drew into the wall mirror, pulled off the bandage, and examined the incised area above his eye. Scabbing up on the edges. It looked like someone had carved a clean arc with a V-gauge. He replaced the dressing.

The only sound at the other end was quiet clacking.

"Is that Millennium Falcon the same as our old version? Maybe a few new characters? BB-8?" He needed another cigarette and a drink. Lit one. Poured one. He knew he'd be doing a lot of talking. Cze carried the iPad to the bed and laid back on the headboard. "It'd be great if Chewie's bowcaster really worked. What's that cockpit look like?"

There was no response from Decker, only the sounds of him stacking the bricks, stud upon stud shuffling. Hands. Partial legs. Breathing.

"Well, maybe next time. What's Grandma been feeding you for breakfast?"

The boy didn't respond.

"Maple bacon folded in toast, a bowl of cornflakes and milk?"

More silence.

"You're eating, though. Right?"

Clacking sounds.

"The Summit Series is on Netflix. When I get home, maybe we can watch that together again. Okay? When I get home."

The silence always hurt Cze. He hurt for his son. For the loss of his legs. He hurt for what had become of their relationship since Maddie abandoned them. His head ached. He needed some pills.

"What's it like there?" mumbled Decker.

Cze sat upright, slowly pressed his cigarette into the plate. The boy didn't talk a lot. When he did, Cze paid attention.

"Uh, what's it like here? Quiet mostly. But there's a river. Fishing. Trout. Lots of different rocks. Trees. Some animals. I saw some deer wandering around one night. Dark because hardly any street lights. They were standing like statues. I screamed a little when I saw them."

Decker laughed softly.

Cze took in the boy's laugh. They hadn't laughed together much since his mother had run off.

"Peeyum, peeyum."

Cze recognized Decker's sound for guns firing. "Liquidating?"

"Yup."

"Storm troopers?"

"Nope," he said. "You."

"Miss you, Deck." What he really meant was that he missed the old life. He had hoped for a response. Nothing.

⌇

"YOU MUST HAVE something by now."

Cze could see Smith from the nose down. Everything in the dark but his teeth.

"You have to adjust your frame. Tilt. First time on Zoom?"

"No, second. Sheehan set me up. Seems he's a bit of a technical wiz. At his age, who knew?"

"Get him to set up your lighting."

"He's gone now. On assignment. There's a terrorist threat on Parliament Hill."

"I heard."

"*Domestic* — that's all we know so far." Smith tented his fingers. "Wozniak, Warren Johnson would like to meet you after the story is done. Fly you out to Toronto. The owners want to fast-track you to a larger market. You're earmarked for grooming. So, when you get back here. After the story is done."

"Wants to see me?"

"Your future is golden. You're marketable in every way."

"Marketable?"

"Let's face it. Communications is a surface business. You have a commanding on-air presence. Multi-demographic-friendly. We'll keep your real name as it will appeal to diverse communities — immigrants, refugees, ethnicities, old, young. International potential. You're fucking sharp. Jesus, you'll probably end up owning the company."

Cze laid a feather on the dresser. He had a collection of ten feathers of different sorts and sizes. All pure white — well, actually eggshell colour, that somehow went beyond the known concept of colour. The feathers seemed to be ethereal — nothing from this world. "He's growing feathers."

"What did you say?"

"Feathers. They seem to be falling off him."

"I don't understand."

"Well. Yeah. Dead birds, crows everywhere. Feathers everywhere."

"So let me clarify. You think he's growing feathers? Or are the feathers from the dead birds."

"Uh, I-I'm not sure."

"You're either one lucky journalistic son-of-a-bitch right now, or you're crazy. And if the latter, I'm in deep shit."

Cze threw his iPad on the bed. Tired. Depressed. Guilt. All of the above. He shot back the whiskey and lay on the bed. Stared at the ceiling. Unspooled.

Smith slowly rose from his Ekornes and wandered to the window. Cold. Empty. His Mercedes alone in the parking lot. His mind on work. Something was not quite right. In all his years in journalism, this, *this story*, had mythical potential. But somehow it felt unhooked.

13

日 の 出 に

at sunrise: *hinode ni*

Good morning. Good morning to you.

What that means?

Kousuke waited patiently for the sun to rise. A favourite thing. He'd accumulated a list of favourite things in this lifetime — the list ever changing. Some items had been scratched off the list but returned years later; some had always been part of the list and moved up and down in priority. He was conscious of keeping it updated. Just in case death came again.

Natural light always, you know, in the top five. Early-morning skies just between the darkness and the full-blown day were perpetual listees — they were on the heels of evening golds. Kousuke thought that miracles either happened or were cultivated during this short timeframe when the light imposed upon the dark, when the stretch of cloud is tinged with pinks, blues, and greys. The saturation of colour increased and cast that indescribable light that Kousuke was sure had healing properties. He'd study the light as it traversed the interiors. It travelled across the ceiling, through water in the glass, across the oak floor, over angles of the doors. Kousuke traced the calibration of hue in the sky, the constellation of stellars that reflected from the bedroom's crystal doorknob — he followed the light until the moment that light beauty would apex. There it is, there it is, his pulse would read, and then gone. Why do you have to watch that light? Because that kind of light would never be seen in such a configuration ever again.

He had a plan this morning and it was time to set up. But he had to hurry. For the sky was moving, the syrupy light beginning to butter the walls. He started his counting — counting gave him pace and purpose, allowed singular focus. One breath, two breaths. The only distraction he permitted was noticing the bee that lit upon the sill, then another. Another. Yet another. He reached back into his memory. Bees. He forgot to count as his mind wandered to the incident from long ago. And it couldn't be helped: his mind strayed from the light.

He didn't have time for books. His head and hands needed to focus on the farming. But he couldn't stay away from the books. If only he had more time. As it was, time he should have spent sleeping was spent learning the English language and reading books.

He had befriended the old librarian who was also a retired teacher. Her name was Mrs. Carver. Kousuke never let her down in keeping the books in good condition and returning them when he was supposed to. The brick façade of the library and its wired fencing disappeared behind him as he rounded the corner of 13th Street North. Kousuke passed church lady Mrs. Sinclair's Victorian house. She was humming a church song on her porch as she watered her plants, then went back inside. She'd led the congregation in song at that Christian church that he'd wandered into one day and promptly been ushered out of. But they said he could sit outside and listen on Sundays. So he did. The song stuck in his head, 'What a friend we have in Je-sus,' that was as far as he could remember. Over time he simply shaped his own religion that was a combination of old family photos, nature, and God is good. Though his sentiments on these matters were ever evolving.

He kicked lightly at the old rusted barrel the church lady kept beneath the lilac bushes because he was curious about what kind of sound it would make. He regretted it immediately. The barrel hummed as the bees rose up out of it like smoke. Kousuke began to run sideways, his arms re-clutching his stack of library books. The swarm slanted toward him and strangely took on the shape of Kousuke's shadow. A few broke from the network and scouted the top of his book stack.

He slowly and gently put the armful of books down on the ground. He'd rather be stung, he thought, than damage any of the books. His eyes fixed upon the *swarm of bees as they slowly approached him. The bees forming a living bag swallowing* The Wonderful Wizard of Oz, Four Footed Friends, *and* Micrographia. *He couldn't leave them. But what could he do? He lifted his hands slowly to the sky and spread his fingers straight as arrows. The bees dispersed. Some of them spiralled up and flew in different directions. But a few fell like pieces of broken glass. Kousuke picked these bees up by their delicate wings. Managed one by one to place them gently in his palm. With books in one arm and dead bees balancing in hand, he continued on his way.*

The pink light began to fill the room. It would last a few minutes. He sat on the stool and stared with fear and excitement at the mirror. The light washed over him. The sublime beauty of the wings bordered on perversity. But when they met the light Kousuke thought that in so many years he had never felt the feeling of home more than at this very moment. He knew that some animals could regenerate body parts. But this? He could only attribute this to some sort of uncharted neural reprogramming due to his age.

The luminous feeling was short-lived as the electrocution came again. He fell to the floor on his hands and knees and began to wail. Then he curled into fetal position, the soft feathers beneath his body. He tried hard to think of something ordinary. "A," he said. "B." It was a comfort. "C, D, E, F, G..." And he fell asleep.

14

薄暗い幽霊

dim spirit: *usugurai yūrē*

Smoke, fog, or imminent rain.

It was difficult to say.

The partially veiled sun was a soft pink over the wheat fields. Cze couldn't believe how beautiful the landscape was in this eerie overcast splendour. The ethereal backdrop seemed to lull him into a place of mystic timelessness. There was some noticeable discomfort, too — his throat had become scratchy and a mild headache palmed.

"What took you?"

"I had to drive up the road a way and park on a side-out beyond your land."

"Why didn't you just park behind that cluster of pines like I told you?"

"Because there was a large man circling that maple tree in your backyard chasing away all the crows. Looked like he was on a mission. I just didn't know what he'd do if he saw me." The creeping didn't sit well with Cze. In fact, the reason for his being with the old man in the first place was now in question.

Kousuke's face soured. "Saunder. My great-great-great-granddaughter's husband. Regrettable. I am convinced he hypnotized her into marrying him. *Sumimasen*. Sorry. Sorry. Where Anya is concerned, I admit to allowing sentiment to slink into my judgement. Anyways, he wants to cut down the tree. He thinks it's got blight." Kousuke looked out at the maple. "Never did trust that —" Kousuke struggled to find the name on his tongue. "What was his name again?"

"Saunder. His name is Saunder. You don't trust this relative and yet you trust me? You don't even know me."

"Let me assure you, life was rather boring before you arrived. You're interesting. I think we share unusual loss and pain somehow. But trust?"

"I'm a stranger."

"Well, as I say, I wouldn't go quite that far. And you're not quite a stranger. No offence but you're educated — a product of Western pedagogical assumptions. Which you can't help. Me? I've had a lifetime of contamination, fights, broken bones, bloodshed resulting from that kind of foolishness. You're under consideration as far as I'm concerned."

Cze couldn't figure if he was astounded or amused by this old man. Both.

"I've got a bat at hand if you don't pan out. Oldest batter for the Coaldale Nisei Cubs," Kousuke proclaimed, poking his index finger at his chest. "Once, long ago."

Kousuke strayed as he gazed up at the sky. He pretended to gently tear pieces of *washi* and tack them to the horizon. "*Chigiri-e* looks like." There was a fire somewhere on the prairies. Ghosts filled the air. The beauty seemed so glorious that it mitigated the evil. Floating in the air were many hidden transgressions. Something old, something with the history of suffering was burning. Kousuke sneezed countless times. "They're dusting up."

"You can smell the ghosts?"

"Well, at my age, I'm nearly a ghost. They are part of my world."

"Do you believe in ghosts?"

Kousuke pulled a tissue from beneath his many layers of clothing, blew his nose, and changed the subject again. "Your sketchbook is on the table. Look around. There are a lot of crows out there today. Maybe the smoke is keeping them down. Why don't you study some prairie crows? Might be different than your city crows."

"I could."

"Then you'll stay," he decided. A flurry of sneezes followed. "Dine with me tonight. My Anya is bringing soup and *gōya chanpurū* for supper. Do you know *gōya*?"

"No."

"It's the bitter melon. An acquired taste. It's a Ryukyuan medicine food — so bitter it can scare off disease." Kousuke chuckled. "*Nigai.* At precisely five o'clock, you hide until she leaves." A twinkle in Kousuke's eye, as though this were a game.

"I'm not so sure that's a good idea."

Kousuke proceeded out the door. "Bring that box, will you?" Kousuke pointed to the *sanshin* with his cane.

Cze picked up the oblong box while simultaneously tapping at his cell phone.

"All this smoke. There's an old residential school on the Blood Reserve that has been on fire since early this morning. The building appears to have been lost."

"You sure?"

"I checked the news on the internet."

Kousuke whispered. "*Intanet?* What was that again? I know it. *Intanet.*"

"Here, I'll show you," Cze retrieved the iPhone and searched for the clip of the fire. "See?"

Kousuke watched intently with wide eyes. "*Omoshiroi.* It's a wonder."

"Doesn't your family show you?"

"They try to keep me old," he said with a smile. "Anyways, books better. Cze Wozniak. Can you find Okinawa?"

Cze searched the word *Okinawa.* An array of multimedia stories appeared. He played the top video.

Kousuke watched the footage of a peace rally lined with elderly opposing construction of an American military base. He watched with concern as the reporter mentioned a woman named Kokubo, whom he surmised as quite a bit younger than he, maybe over eighty years old. She held a sign. She was being handled by the police. "Kokubo-*obasan.* Shimajiri-*gun.* Must be." They watched as the old woman resisted.

Cze pocketed the phone again. "Internet." He didn't know why he felt the need to clarify that it was internet and not *intanet*. It didn't matter. But maybe the old man would have wanted to know.

"Well, I know anyways. The troubles with American military bases. *Intanet* knows. But I know, too, without *intanet*." He intentionally slowed his speech and carefully said, "With these disrupters, it would take a miracle to preserve the sacred groves and ocean where *kami* have resided as we have known; the gods endure." A moment of glittering critical thinking synchronicity. How he wished Anya had been there to hear him deliver that one sentence. Though she likely wouldn't know what it meant.

It took some time to settle into the chair on the porch. Sitting was just a little awkward now, but still manageable. His banded wings were surprisingly accommodating. He laid the oblong box on his lap. The last time he played the *sanshin* was before the East China Sea. He would sit on the largest of the rocks watching white caps upon white caps roll to the shores where flightless *yambaru kuina* would run along the skim of the waves on the sands. "Happy," he said, reminiscing. For a moment he had found an essay of eternity.

The pain came on suddenly. He tried to dismiss it. He fell. Gripped the leg of the chair. Scanned the sky.

Cze quickly reached for the old man.

Kousuke pushed him away. "Where am I? *Doko?*" He ran his hand along the edge of one of his concealed wings.

A few feathers fell from beneath his clothing then danced across the porch.

One of the feathers caught on Cze's shoe. He picked it up in wonder. Was Kousuke pocketing feathers? Was he wearing them?

"Who am I, now? *Dare? Intanet.* In-ter-net," he said trying to whole himself. It took a bit to find reality.

Cze noticed that Kousuke had stretches of focussed brilliance and then everything would scramble into confusion. It seemed, he would grapple with words: Okinawan and English, Japanese and English, Okinawan and Japanese. Almost as though he didn't know which identity or which word to choose — he gently oscillated between realms. Cze also noted that one of the old man's eccentricities was his apparel. At times incomprehensible. On this hot day, for example, Kousuke wore layers of clothing topped with a coat. Which incidentally cushioned him in the fall.

Kousuke sat very still.

Cze sat quietly on the porch steps and sketched the crows.

They sat this way for some time. No words were exchanged.

After a while Kousuke drew the item from the oblong box. The long neck was elegant. Lacquered black. The body was covered in snakeskin and encased in gold brocade.

Cze stopped sketching. "What is that? It's remarkable."

"It's called a *sanshin. Sō, kore.*" He ran his fingers down the long neck of the *sanshin*. "*Kore wa, tiigaa.*" He tapped at the gold brocade covering the sides of the drum. "*Chiiga.*" He waved his hand over the drum. "*Uma.*" He carefully drew the bone bridge along the python skin and erected it beneath the three strings on the rough drum-skin. He began to tune the strings. "*Bachi.* Ox horn." He slipped the lacquered pick on his finger and began to play. The sound wasn't pure, and that's exactly what made it pure.

It wasn't perfect to Cze's ear, but the way Kousuke sang with the strings was perfect to the senses. It was a chant or a conjuring. He returned to the pencil and paper, this time sketching Kousuke, the crooked fingers on the strings.

After some time Kousuke stopped. "You should bring him here, don't you think? He would like it here."

"Who?"

"Your son."

Cze focussed on the graphite lines and the sound of the pencil dragging on the paper. He never took his eyes off the page. "Did I mention him? I don't remember telling you about my son."

Crows squawked in the cottonwood. The two were content to just sit on the porch. One with pencil and one with *sanshin.*

"Cze Wozniak, you sketch crows." Kousuke stared at nothing in particular for a long while. A smile spread. "You're different. Parts of you soft. Parts of you strong. Mostly broken, though."

"Ha, maybe you're right," Cze said with a smile contemplating this one-hundred-thirty-year-old man who just at this moment said to him *You're different.* He longed for a cigarette. "How did you know I had a son?"

Kousuke clutched the *sanshin*, noted the discolouration of the strings. Dismissed Cze.

"I didn't tell you." Cze caught Kousuke's gaze. His head ached. He needed a drink, pills, a cigarette.

"No." Kousuke looked to Cze and then gave a nod to his left side. "She did."

Cze looked to his side. Of course there was no one.

Kousuke tightened the *karakui*. He knew the tuning would take some time. The pegs often refused to relinquish control.

15

呼 吸

breathe: *kokyū*

"Hey, what if I woke up and you were there beside me? You know, like a pearl? A beautiful pearl. Instead of taking flight, Maddie. I mean, what if I woke up and you were still here?" It was a good place to start writing the story for the newspaper. Here by the water. But it was evident that he lacked focus.

Cze skipped a flat stone, hovered it across the Old Man River and muttered, "He saw you. Knew about Decker, too. Too bad, though, that he couldn't tell me where you'd run off to. Or when, if ever, you were coming back." Cze threw the stones particularly hard with very little finesse — they cut angrily into the water. "He can see things and that scares me. Another thing, I'm pretty damn sure he's growing wings." He kicked over a pile of shale shards to reveal the underside wet with surface ammonite and glittering like the scales of rainbow trout. "Nice." He hated that word, *nice*. "I gotta stop talking to myself."

Cze wandered along the shore beneath the old rail bridge where he'd read that these ancient valleys, the old Blackfoot land, were rife with fossils and even arrowheads if one cared to spend the time digging. He spent some time taking photos of the banks with his long lens, then some panoramas. He wondered how it was possible that he had never seen this area when it was only a day away from Ezra. Decker would love all of this, he thought. He wondered how the wheelchair would manage the terrain — it couldn't, he surmised. But they could find a way. Cze picked up the branch that had washed ashore beside him. He prodded and poked at the clay banks, watched the sapling branch curve and spring from the pressure.

He found a large rock slab, unloaded the backpack from his shoulders, retrieved his iPad, tried the first sentence of his assignment: *An unhastened wisp of lament carried in the dust...* Nope. He tried another line. *Kousuke Kana is the oldest man in the world. He's lived one hundred thirty years and I think he's growing wings.*

Cze didn't know how long he'd been writing on that rock. Long enough for his neck to stiffen up from typing in an arch. It was the cool wind that caused him to look up. Anxiety. He found beyond the blue-sky horizon a bruised army of impatient amorphous clouds. An ominous crescent began to halo above Kousuke's land. Cze quickly set the camera up for lighting conditions that were changing on the fly. He cupped the heavy lens, tilted up, and took some traditional shots. Then some multiple exposures. Various compositions. Strong originals with potential to manipulate in Photoshop. He wanted plenty of raw assets to work with. The sound of the shutter amid the dead stillness was incredible. He breathed the moment in.

⟿

"IT WILL HANG ABOVE for a long while," Kousuke said.

They sat on the porch and watched the sky. "It's more foreboding from the river," Cze said as he inhaled and let the wind take the smoke.

"You got some good photographs?"

"Yes."

For a time they stared at the circling clouds.

"So what was she like?"

"Who?"

"Your wife."

Kousuke considered Cze for a while. "I don't know you well enough to say."

"You saw mine. It's only fair I learn about your wife," Cze said, putting out the cigarette. "Oh, here." He fished a perfectly round flat stone out from his pocket. It was the size of his palm. Gave it to the old man.

"A nice one. Thank you." Kousuke lay the rock on the front porch with the other flat rocks — there were about two dozen in total now near the female *shisa* lion statue. Then he pushed the rocks around with his cane until it was aesthetically pleasing to him. "She was plain," he said. "Emiko was." Kousuke slowly pushed the flat stone to the bottom right near the pink granite. "She was plain as the soups she made bone-stitched together with garden spuds, carrots, and *napa* cabbage." Kousuke moved the ammonite near the blue flat stone and the pink granite stone and made a sub-group. "She was plain as her long gloss of hair tied in a knot at the back of her neck where strands escaped in gentle tendrils about her round face. Emiko had small plain eyes that shone like stars in the night that had come to understand reason. My wife was ordinary. Nothing fancy. She was plain. She was beautiful."

Cze sat on the step of the porch and moved one of the flat rocks that Kousuke had carefully positioned.

"That was a long time ago." Kousuke pushed the rock that Cze had moved back into its position. His cane shook a bit as he moved it. "A long time ago. Go get me the dictionary. It's in the drawer left of the sink. There are more stories about her in the dictionary."

Cze watched the sky as dark clouds continued to march over the foothills. "I don't think there are stories of her in the dictionary," he said quietly.

"No?"

"No."

16

他人

stranger: *tanin*

He fixated on the button she had embroidered.
On her lapel. It was a cat.
"Don't tell the others that he's here, Peck."
"*Ojīsan.* He's a stranger." *Peck.* She'd loved birds when
she was little — had wild bird pets all her life. *Peck.* No one
called her that anymore. Only him. She tried to assess
Kousuke's hooded owl eyes. It had taken a long time for
Anya to come to terms with Kousuke's mental state, which
Dr. Senada called "not quite dementia." She had come to
identify when he was in that *not quite dementia* state. At
first, she tried to dismiss it with the hopes that it would
simply go away. Sometimes it did. Anya zigzagged thoughtfully through university courses like Brain Plasticity and
Memory and even an Education course, Brain and Behaviour
in Teaching, to gain a better understanding of Kousuke's
condition. She scoured literature as part of her effort to
outthink the dementia. She kept losing.

"He's supposed to be here. Not really a stranger."

"No, he's not supposed to be here. Yes, really — he's a stranger." She cradled the *furoshiki* of *chanpurū* and soup in her arm and plucked a sticky note from the wall. Held the paper squared in front of Kousuke. "No strangers allowed," she whispered gently. "Ever." She turned to Cze with a glare. "You're taking advantage of a lonely old man," she accused. "How have you so ably gained this old man's trust? You have skills, Mr. Wozniak."

Cze stood awkwardly. Feeling foolish. Feeling guilty.

"I'm not lonely," Kousuke said. "He is good conversation and a good man. You should know that in this short time I've come to value him. He was a stranger. Now a friend. His character is sound. This friendship is made with sound judgement."

"With this large family," Cze mumbled hesitantly, "he should be anything but lonely."

"Are you saying we are neglecting him?" Anya tried to gain eye contact with Cze. "If you weren't sneaking around, presuming to know all, you'd see the schedule of attention."

"Scheduled attention? Like an assignment?"

"You're full of it, you know?" Anya said. "Assignment. You should know the definition of assignment. For he is an assignment to you, isn't he?"

Cze looked at Kousuke with a sheep shit of a smile, lowered his gaze.

"Stranger," she said, boring accusingly into Cze's incredible eyes. "Stranger, he's let you in because of his dementia."

Cze countered in almost a whisper, "He is quite capable. Sharp. Witty. I'd be hard-pressed to appropriate —"

"Really? Watch this. *Ojīsan*, what is the largest island in the Ryukyuan chain?"

"What?"

"Standard questions. Please indulge me and the stranger." Anya continued to glare at Cze. "You're unethical — easy enough to prove."

"You're testing my cognition, Peck? My sanity? How dare you. You're trying to embarrass me."

"No. But I know the questions Dr. Senada would ask. I am trying to protect you. What is the largest island in the Ryukyuan chain?"

"Not only is this elder abuse, but an offence to my pride." Kousuke pointed at Anya. "You are humiliating me in front of my friend."

"He's not a friend of yours. He's a stranger. I could care less about your indignation. I am trying to protect you." Anya proceeded to quickly write a new sticky note: CZE WOZNIAK = STRANGER. "Your memory is short. Perception distorted. You're old. Something in your brain malfunctions from time to time resulting in bad behaviour — hippocampal idling resulting in synaptic misfire." Anya stood firm. "Never mind, I'm just going to call the police."

"Goddammit. You see how stubborn she is?" Kousuke mumbled to Cze. "I swear, sometimes you seem to forget that I am a living, breathing creature and not simply a human subject for your neuroscience undergraduate pseudo-research."

Anya was fixed. "Honestly, *ojīsan.* And I'll take back the textbooks that I've lent you. They are due at the library."

"Okay. Okay. You're showing off, Anya. However, carry on with your interrogation. And if I shine, we three dine."

"No deal."

"Oh, it's a deal, Peck."

"Don't call me Peck, *ojīsan.*"

"You ask what's the largest island in the Ryukyuan chain? Okinawa, of course," said Kousuke.

"How old are you?"

Kousuke sighed. "Fine. I'm one hundred thirty years old."

"Where were you born?"

"I was born in the potter's village of Yomitan on the island of Okinawa. The largest island of the Ryukyuan chain. Where multiple cultures engaged in a rich community of oceanic trade. Where strangers were welcome with open arms." Kousuke playfully eyed Anya. "An island that enjoyed nature's harvest for joy and medicinal value and where the arts flourished. Where farmers and fishermen danced to little gods." Kousuke stared hawkishly at Anya. Lucidity evident. "Ironically, the island of peace suffered immeasurably during the Second World War. It was used by the Japanese military as the stage for the largest land, air, and amphibious battle of all time. It became a bloodbath for soldiers and islanders alike — surely a rustbelt that would scream 'Here, this is the timeframe where the island cried.' One of every four civilians lost their lives as they ran openly like bugs amid the rain of artillery — well over a hundred thousand civilians died in just over eighty days. My parents along with two sisters perished when a hand grenade was thrown into the cave. Along with other islanders and soldiers who were forced to the southern tip at the end of the battle, my eldest sister jumped off the rock cliffs of Manube. I was here in Canada. I live. They all died. My guilt is sometimes unbearable. My name is Kousuke. I come from a humble island cradled in the cobalt blue of the East China Sea. Oh, and my favourite hockey player of all time is Number 4, Bobby Orr."

Yeah, Bobby Orr. The old man's voice was so calm. He was luminous. Though he had a curious aversion to luminous. Suspicious of it, even.

Anya's eyebrow arched — there was a glint in her eye. She smiled.

"Old man wants very much to keep this friend."

A new incredible sense of shame washed over Cze's pre-existing incredible sense of shame. "I sh-should go," he said quietly, closing his sketchbook. He once again struggled with his conscience. "Thank you," he said to Kousuke and in his awkwardness found himself bowing slightly. He couldn't bring himself to look at the old man at the risk of his seeing the guilt related to the deceptive intentions upon which the relationship was built. He decided at that moment that he wouldn't be back.

"Cze Wozniak, you need to sit." Kousuke placed his hand on the young man's shoulder. He took the dishes from

Anya's hands and placed them on the counter. "And you need to sit, too," he urged. "*Suware.* Remember our deal, we three dine."

"You and your deals," Anya said. She stood rooted on the plank flooring for a moment, then proceeded to set three places at the table.

Kousuke went to his cold storage and brought out a bottle of *awamori.* "This is for special occasions."

"What are you trying to do, *ojīsan?* I don't like him. He's an opportunist." She turned to Cze. "Why would you befriend an old man? Because you know exactly who he is — the oldest man on the planet. You are a journalist cloaked as a friend. Worse than a stranger."

Cze sank.

"Are you? Just admit it."

The silence said it all.

Kousuke slowly placed the *awamori* on the kitchen counter. Awaited Cze's answer.

Cze stared out to the setting sun. "Well, you've got me there," he said quietly. "I've been sent by the media." He turned to Kousuke with remorse.

Kousuke nodded somewhat knowingly. "*Ah sou, desu ne.*"

Cze reached for his Bruins hat. "There was a point when it became friendship though. Th-there was something. I just ended up liking you."

"Stay. Share some food first," Kousuke said, reading every nuance. He had no doubt. "*Tabenasai.*"

"*Ojīsan!*" Anya said with a quiet fury.

"Allow an old man," Kousuke said sadly. Pulled out a chair and pushed Cze down into it. "*Suware.* I insist. You owe me."

Cze sat.

"Indulge me." Kousuke stared at Anya with conviction. "Listen, I understand that I have moments flecked with mental illness, flocked even. I understand that my faculties are in drastic decline. I understand that you think the isolation of my growing dementia has affected my judgement here." Ever so quietly. "Bear with me on this."

"What is it?" Anya glared at Cze, then Kousuke. "A reporter and the oldest man in the world. A relationship built on trust? Circumstances make that impossible." She posed her rhetorical questions and answers to no one in particular, then turned to the kitchen counter. "Why is he here, *ojīsan?* There is no value."

Great value, Kousuke thought to himself.

Dark clouds continued to convene, coruscate with quiet fires, and crawl silently across the sky.

17

暴露

the reveal: *bakuro*

Refrain from gestures.

Not here. The feeling was strong.

Too late.

"Mrs. Wozniak, my name is Mack Smith. I'm the publisher of the *Ezra Herald*. Your son Cze works for me. He's on assignment for me."

The woman stood tall and firm. Spoke through the screen door. "Is something wrong? Is he okay?" She wiped her hands on the dishcloth that hung over her left shoulder.

"No, there's nothing wrong. As it turns out, I just wanted to — May I come in?"

Sonia Wozniak stood at the door for a time.

Smith fumbled for a business card and held it against the screen in front of Sonia.

She slowly unlocked and opened the door.

"A pleasure to meet you." Nails manicured. Teeth gleaming.

Sonia Wozniak said nothing.

Smith noticed what a striking resemblance there was between mother and son. The same blue eyes, unusually thick hair, and solid frame. Physically striking in a classical sense, but like her son, she seemed paradoxically unaware, even bore a cultivated notion of anti-beauty. Which Smith quickly dismissed as ridiculous.

He handed her a fresh olive and dill loaf from that quaint bakery near the office. It was soft on the inside and crusty on the outside — just the way he liked it. He was almost inclined to keep it for himself.

Upon entering the home, Smith spotted a large canvas black-and-white photo on the wall by the entry, an aerial shot of a large farm and walked toward it.

"That's a spectacular property. Is that your farm?"

"Was."

He wondered who would live on such a large stretch of land. Hutterite colonies in the area, Smith thought — maybe Mennonite? He got tangled in inner discourse for a bit, then carried on with his uninvited exploration of the Wozniak home.

He stopped at the alcove bay off the living room. A photograph collection of a boy and Cze rowed on a mantle. A small reading area full of books. Awards and certificates hung on the wall. Recognition for writing, English honours, significant scholarships, academic medals. All Sonia's doing as she was intensely proud of Cze.

"Did he always have a gift for writing?"

"Always had pen and paper in hand. Yes. What do you want, Mr. Smith?" Sonia said bluntly. "I'm afraid I'll be leaving to pick my grandson up from physio in about fifteen minutes."

"Grandson? Physio?"

Sonia regretted saying the words *grandson* and *physio* to this man.

"I just wanted to check in on you. Make sure everything is okay while Cze is away on assignment. Since I was the one responsible for sending him away, I thought I should."

"That's not necessary. I don't even know you."

He disregarded her response. And therein was one of the keys to Smith's success — deflection and persistence. "He's a brilliant young man. I knew it from the first interview. He rose above the rest. Has he kept in touch with you? Has he mentioned the story he's chasing? An old man?"

"No."

"Talk of birds?"

"No."

"What a lovely seating area. Carpets from Istanbul?"

"Canadian Tire."

Smith thought the visit wasn't a complete waste of time. But nearly. The woman was ice. Nothing. No word of wings.

"Again, thank you for your hospitality."

An uncomfortable silence.

"Uh, here's my business card." He presented it for the second time. "Call me if you need anything." Sonia glanced at her wristwatch. For a second time he slipped the card back into his pocket.

Through the screen she watched the well-dressed giant of a man wave back to her as he got into his shiny black Mercedes.

She locked the door.

18

昇天

ascension: *shōten*

The ceaseless wind. It crept around one side of the house like a caress and then proceeded to buffet the other violently. Kousuke found strange comfort in the sound of the wind. He had experienced varying degrees of prairie windstorms and had witnessed a semi-trailer full of cattle fold into a Pincher Creek ditch; the roof of a horse stable gyrate its way to Iron Springs; and century-old pines uproot and then halve homes. So this particular gusting wind wasn't of great concern. Inside, the three dined.

"This soup is from pork ribs," said Anya.

"*Soba* noodles, this time, instead of spaghetti?" Kousuke said, slurping eagerly.

"Yes."

"*Kombu maki?*"

"Yes."

"Baby bok choy and scallion slivers?"

"Yes."

"Sliced *kamaboko?*"

"Yes."

"Soft-boiled eggs with *shoyū* drizzle, black pepper sprinkle?"

"Yes."

"Small side of *umeboshi* and rice?"

"Yes."

"*Gōya* slivers, tofu, egg stir-fry?"

"Yes."

"An *umeboshi* a day. They say." Kousuke laughed.

"It's all so good," Cze said, managing the noodles with his chopsticks. "That *gōya* is interesting."

"Have more," Kousuke said. "There's plenty."

Anya glanced at the old man. "You're hunching that odd way again. Are you winded?"

"Hm?" Kousuke said stretching for time. The wings were beginning to weigh him down.

"Your back. You're slouching. Or —" Anya was slightly alarmed. "Is something wrong with your back?"

"Anya, I'm old. Optics and posture are the least of my worries," Kousuke grinned. "Besides, who am I to impress?"

"Well, there's Mrs. Nagasano. At ninety-six years old, you'd be robbing the cradle. But I think she has an eye for you."

Cze watched the old man straighten his spine. Then look on the floor beneath him for feathers.

"Um, what exactly is your assignment?" Anya eyed Kousuke with suspicion first then Cze.

"You're both writers," the old man said. "What are you writing?"

"I asked first," Anya protested.

Kousuke broke the stalemate. "You go first, Peck."

"Don't call me that."

"Go. Say what."

Anya stared at her soup for a while. She wasn't sure whether to talk about her writing. She rarely did. "Um. There's a story. About a mound of bones. Sacred ground is being dragged into the ocean. No one is listening." Anya wasn't sure why she was even telling the concept to Cze.

"I'm listening," Kousuke said with a small smile. Cze nodded at Kousuke in agreement.

Anya looked at the pair in wonder. Within such a short period, how could they have become so closely allied? Why should she tell them? Nevertheless, she did.

Cze noticed her face soften in the candlelight. Skin shone. Eyes sparkled. The way she spoke of her writing project captivated him.

"Sorry. What?"

"She asked you to talk about yourself," Kousuke responded. "Where are you? Who are you, Cze Wozniak?"

"Uh, can I just say this is amazing soup? My mom makes cabbage borscht. That is our family soup."

"One day you can bring me. Right now? Tell your story."
Kousuke leaned back on the chair as best he could. "Go."

"Well, my grandparents were farmers," Cze said. "I'm the

odd one out, I guess. Like you, Anya, I am fascinated by words. And lines, too."

"Words and drawing, huh? What else of interest?"

"Well, I'm going through a bit of a withdrawal. You know, the usual twenty-first century rehab fits and starts."

"Oh."

"Yup."

Cze watched the light stretch across the walls.

"Any other, uh, matters of interest?" Anya repeated.

"Lego is of great interest. Cze Wozniak, it seems has a son," Kousuke said, gathering the last of his rice into a small pile at the edge of his bowl. "A boy who likes to build things."

Cze poured green tea for Kousuke, Anya, and then himself. "Yeah, my boy, he's got an incredible curiosity for geology, and strange taste for world cuisine. He actually built a sushi platter out of Lego once."

"I would like see something like that," said Kousuke.

"Your wife?" Anya cradled the green tea cup.

Cze took a turn back to gazing at the wall. "Hm. My wife." He considered for a bit before responding. "Aw hell, why not? There was an accident. My wife lost her mind and then vanished. My son lost his legs. He doesn't have his legs. Lost all his friends. Our father-and-son relationship is really broken. I-I think we're floundering in the shallows."

Anya and Kousuke were still. Kousuke looked down at the tip of his chopsticks and how close they were to the remaining kernels of rice. Anya stared unwaveringly into Cze's eyes, into the deep.

For the rest of the evening, the wind.

After dinner, Kousuke announced he was off to his green-house to untangle the tomato vines and to give a *sanshin* performance to his statues.

"Statues?"

"You obviously haven't seen the greenhouse. Not what you'd expect."

"Yeah?"

"A lifetime of work. Trying so hard to carve out living flesh. Okinawan civilians during the war. Guilt."

"Why?"

"For being here, and not there."

The candlelight brushed wild things across the barren walls and ceilings. Cze watched her slender, elegant hands tell a story. He watched her perfectly shaped mouth over teeth that were imperfect in the most perfect way softening sentences composed of words like *caustic, acerbic,* and *corrosive.* She swept back her crown of hair and its multitude of browns. Tendrils that escaped from the topknot gently framed her face. Her hazel eyes lit up and rimmed gold when she spoke about writing and translations — about the *hiragana, katakana,* and *kanji.* He turned his gaze now and then to the book stacks on floor, to the dimming treelines, and to the small pool of broth that remained in his bowl — any diversion in effort to resist the urge to stare too long at her. He wanted to make her laugh. He wondered what she looked like when she laughed.

"*Hajimemashite. Cze desu.*"

"Do you understand? How much of the Japanese language do you understand?"

"*Hai, nihongo wakarimasu. Sukoshi.* A little," he said. Immediately, he saw what a mistake he had made. Rather than make Anya laugh, Cze managed to arouse more suspicion.

She cupped her green tea. "We both know you're profiting from an unfair advantage," Anya said looking out at the sky. Residue. The wind had changed direction and was sending some of the smoky air into the house. She rose to jog shut the muntins. They were old like everything else about this house.

"What do you mean exactly?"

"He's old. Lonely. You've befriended him. You've got an agenda," she said with controlled quiet. "Who are you? Tell me the truth. Obviously, you gained his friendship under false pretenses."

Cze was bewildered by her. He didn't want to be. He was.

"Who are you? Tell me," Anya repeated.

He retreated, slumped, then casually leaned back in his chair. "I'm a reporter. I'm a fucking reporter." He stood up. "But after time he became my friend. I gotta go."

Just then there was a knock at the door. Anya jumped. Her green tea spilled on the stack of Russians, Tolstoy on top. The door swung open bringing in wild night air that blew the sticky notes about. *LOCK DOORS* flew to the table, *AVOID PROCESSED MEATS* flew up high then settled precariously on top of the toaster, *DON'T EVER TALK TO STRANGERS* flew right out the door.

Cze could instantly feel the friction mount. Saw the change in her.

"Damn windstorm barrelling over the prairies." Saunder stood at the doorway squinting from the dust. "Coming home?" He was big, broad-shouldered. Over six feet tall. Features that could pass for celebrity, a typical handsome leading man — chiselled jaw, dark brooding eyes. He filled — or rather blocked — the entry. Once he was in the house, cramped. "Thought I'd walk you home." He'd expected to see Kousuke at the kitchen table, not this stranger.

"Cze Wozniak," he said extending a hand. Side by side they were nearly the same build. Cze with a lot less bulk.

"I'm surprised. Kousuke doesn't usually have visitors."

"A friend of *ojīsan*," Anya said.

"A friend," Saunder echoed.

There was something, Cze thought. Something taut.

"I'll be home soon," Anya said. She curved away.

"Actually, storm warning. And seems that pack of coyotes is howling about. Best I walk you home. Here, I brought this."

He held a jacket out for her to slip into. Accidentally dropped it to the floor. Picked it up again with a shake and again held it open for her.

Anya pushed her chair under the table. Saunder slowly wrapped the coat around her. She stiffened. He slowly pulled her hair out from beneath the collar. She became absent. Then he brushed some strands away from her face. She simply looked down. "Tell him goodbye for me," she said, nodding toward the greenhouse.

Together, Cze thought, they were the most physically beautiful couple he'd ever seen. Saunder seemed to care. But did he? This man, Cze thought, didn't fit with these people.

"I'm on way out, too," Cze said. Tucked books under his arm, reached for knapsack, and at the same time flicked the puddle of tea off *Anna Karenina*. The three made their way out to the dusk. Thunder rolled in the distance. "I'll say my goodbyes to Kousuke."

"Tell him I'll visit in the morning," said Anya. Her husband close at her heels, almost corralling her, and sneaking looks at her with what Cze thought was a cold glint.

Cze was certain he saw through a crack in Saunder's veneer. Ducking. Several cracks. He just needed some more time with him in order to discover that he was indeed a certified prick. "I will. I'll tell him."

Over his shoulder, Cze saw Saunder grab Anya's arm forcefully and then they disappeared into the night. The man unnerved Cze. But he was not about to get into an entanglement based on instinct. Besides, none of his business. He couldn't help but think she'd looked like one of those birds that lay lifeless on Kousuke's ground that first day they'd met — submitting to the mercy of the dive.

The wind whipped Anya's hair about. She tried to pull it back out of her face, but Saunder had a firm hold. "My arm," Anya whispered. He knew how to hurt her without it showing. She had tried to keep the secret of being in this web of abuse for so long, mostly to protect Kousuke, that she whispered even in the pitch of the prairie night though there was no one around to hear her.

"What the fuck was that? A candlelit dinner with a stranger? Alone?" Saunder's voice was hard.

"*Ojīsan* was in his greenhouse. I don't suppose you'd believe me if I told you that nothing was happening. Trust me."

"Trust you?" He was almost dragging her along now for it was impossible for her to assume his pace.

She tried to break free.

"Quit squirming," Saunder hissed and squeezed her arm like a vise.

She began to whimper.

"Cry," he said. "No one can hear you." He raised his hand.

She shielded her face.

Lightning struck and the prairies lit up incandescent — exposing sage bushes, poplars, tall fescue, fence lines, and in the distance the flank of the foothills for a split second. At that moment, Anya managed to break free. She ran but didn't get far and was quickly overtaken. Pushed to the ground. Like an animal Saunder straddled her and tore at the front of her blouse.

"Is this what you wanted from him?"

She tried to twist away but couldn't move. He was on top of her. His weight. She struggled to breathe.

Suddenly Cze's cold voice cut through the night. "Let her go." Once he situated, he understood all of it. The darkness.

They were all at the same visual disadvantage — collectively stirring up the dark side of the storm. "Let her go."

They stood in the corpse of the night.

Backlit defined.

19

てぃんさぐぬ花

the balsam flowers: *tinsagu nu hana*

Kousuke's greenhouse sanctuary was a magnificent haven of
sculptures and of growing things. Tribute to Emiko and the
island. Variable measures of guilt, longing and grounding
at any given time multiplied by two. Time One. He'd had
plenty of time to contemplate the loss of Emiko — the only
woman who had known him. She had cared deeply for him.
She brought the island to him. And this may be something
only an immigrant understands: she brought the island to
him when he believed he was alone. Time Two. He'd had
plenty of time to accept the horror of *tetsu no bofu,* the
violent *wind of steel,* and with that the emotions conjured.
Absence from the island.

   The act of sculpting combined both pain and joy, which
when intertwined are a measure of the powerful and extraordinary. The stone family. Beneath the seven-foot hibiscus
tree a barefooted grandmother carrying a baby on her back,
a *nemaki* concealing her weary face. Down the aisle amid the

rows of tomato vines a girl frozen in flight looked fearfully over her shoulder while cinching her windblown kimono. And at the other end of the greenhouse beneath the hanging baskets of fuchsia-coloured Wave petunias was a young boy guiding a crippled old man.

All around, dust and rocks tapped impatiently at the house of glass. Overhead, Kousuke could see the pink light pulsing within the menacing cloud. It morphed into one cryptic shape and then another. Churned. The wind on the ground had suddenly subsided. Stillness. Dead silence. He knew it wasn't right. Then the cloud spawned a funnel, then another, and another. The three rooted blindly about for a while, and then came together as one furious corkscrew.

The greenhouse began to heave. The sheet glass that had only a week or so prior been replaced spidered and suddenly exploded into a galaxy of shards. The carefully re-tended vegetables and flowers vacuumed up into the cosmos. Again. Then the metal frame of the greenhouse rocked and soon followed the path of the plants. A couple of the barrier trees were simultaneously uprooted, leaving gaping cavities in the ground — those that remained were ravished and flayed of their bark. The statues were immovable at first, shook, and then rose straight up like rockets. The main house was left untouched. But the greenhouse was gone. It was as though nothing had ever existed in that place. There.

20

戦い
battle: *tatakai*

With a physical fight you step from civilized into shadow worlds. You don't quite believe it's happening. Perhaps it's a movie. In Cze's case he was only semi-prepared for such a situation. In the shadow world Cze had been bullied as a child at his school for being different — a stutterer. Like Kousuke, he fell into the category of outsider. While Kousuke transferred his energies to the land, Cze learned how to transmute negative energies and pain onto the page, into writing. He could process a bullying episode into poetry, a punch in the gut into prose. That was his power and that is what carried him through academics and life. But the diverse layers, the ones that mattered in the moment, included the forced fistfights with his father who in alcoholic tirades would press the boy to defend himself. In order to avoid physical confrontation, Cze learned to be in the right places around the house at the right times. But here in the night storm on the wide-open prairies, where the buffalo once grazed, where there was wild in the air and no dark stairwell to hide in — he was clearly in deep shit.

Lightning stretched across the sky like a string of firecrackers barbed-wiring the clouds. Those moments that lit up the composition were the most terrifying. Revealing Caravaggio-esque frames of Saunder snapping his head to Cze while attacking Anya. Then, another illumination of Saunder circling Cze like prey. Anticipation. A new and wondrous hunger. Or the most horrific snapshot of all when the torched horizon revealed nothing — absolutely no trace.

The first blow came suddenly to the back of Cze's head. He'd learned how to take a punch as a child, but that was long ago. It jolted his entire world. The second and third bats were to the right ear. Followed by a fisted swat to the face. Cze staggered backwards from the concussive force. He was officially in that shadow world once again.

"You're going to have to do better than that." Saunder grabbed Cze around the neck. "This is going to be fucking easy." Tightened the grip as though preparing to twist a lid off. "I'm going to break your neck."

As another network connected the dots across the sky, Cze felt a surge of adrenalin, and from the headlocked position grabbed Saunder's leg and took him down hard. They both rose quickly and then attacked each other at the same time. Driven by emotion, Saunder thrashed about while Cze became more patient and found his fight rhythm. After a series of calculated blows, he struck Saunder in the jaw, causing the big man to stagger and tilt. One more punch finally toppled him.

Thunder drummed while another lightning flash revealed Saunder reaching for a large fist-sized rock. Cze caught the stone punch on the left side of the head and across the brow. He fell to the ground. Blood pooled.

"Stop!" Anya screamed. "Stop."

"This is all your fault," he said breathing hard. He swatted her with his bloodied hand. "See? It's your fault."

21

夜空

the night sky: *yozora*

The storm sees things differently.

Anya blinked. She was bleary-eyed. She thought she was either dreaming or dying. She was so battered that she didn't feel pain anymore. All she knew was the night was black.

Saunder squinted, his face contorted in confusion. He was taken aback by the figure. How? "Where the hell did *you* come from?"

The lightning continued to flash around them. The thunder so loud, it shook the ground.

Saunder smiled like a devil. "You've never liked me have you, old man?"

Silence.

"You know accidents can happen on a night like this," Saunder said quietly. "And there's nothing you can do about it." He jerked Anya to and fro like a rag doll. She was practically unconscious. "How much do I stand to gain with the both of you gone? Disappearing during a tornado wouldn't be investigated as murder necessarily. Would it? What are you going to do about it, old —" Saunder spun around and tried to find Kousuke. He'd disappeared.

Lightning penetrated the pitch black. All that could be seen was a dark, ambiguous shape above. It swooped down from the sky. Dialed right at Saunder. For a microsecond, Saunder felt the cool caress of a wall of feathers brush against his face and body. A shudder of indescribable fear coursed through his body. Kousuke? But rather than impact him, the creature took an abrupt hairpin turn upward. In riveted silence Saunder watched the bird — for it was some sort of gigantic bird — commanding the thunderous night. It soared with horrific majesty across the electric sky. The sound of flight filled the air. Saunder didn't know which way to run. The creature dove again. Accelerated. It carved around Saunder and then gently scooped up Anya. At that instant a violent crack of thunder reverberated. Like a symphony, lightning struck in every direction. Then one strike crescendoed to an ear-splitting crackle before it entered Saunder through the top of his head, imprinted a venous series of Lichtenburg figures against the canvas of the night, and exited out his left heel. Fingertips charred, hair singed, skin seared. Smoke curled elegantly off the body as though a candle scarcely snuffed.

22

欲

greed: *yoku*

"It's frightening, Smith, to think that you're overseeing one of the country's leading communications outlets. You are multimedia. You have the power of production. Shape lives, destroy them."

"Listen, flattery will get you nowhere." Smith's worst fears and suspicions about his prodigy were beginning to surface — Cze held left-wing ideologies. Johnson had questioned Smith on the decision to give this assignment to a relative rookie. A subversive — why hadn't he seen? This story was squarely on Smith's shoulders, and it was quickly becoming a disaster. Proximity to being ousted from his new position resulted in panic. "How soon can we expect to see something? And what of the wings? Has he turned into a bird, then?" Smith was astonished those words and questions actually came out of his mouth. Desperation evident. He stopped, stepped back, and took a critical look at the pitiful situation at hand. And quickly Smith

shifted back to his natural cup of tea and known reality —
privilege.

"Oh, by the way, I've got a box of Insignia cigarettes here
for you. Johnson just came back from Mumbai. The best
smoke experience in the world."

"I quit."

"What do you mean you quit? You mean smoking?"

23

新たな始まり
new beginning: *aratana hajimari*

A true vanishing.

Not an imagined. True.

Anya couldn't quite understand what had happened. The doctors and nurses at the Prairie Regional Hospital had told her that she would be there for another week, and that many of the hospital beds were occupied with countless others besides them who had been injured by the thunderstorm — twelve deaths in total, and two vanishings. Two *vanishings*.

"It's a strange story, isn't it?"

"Yes."

"Are we taking it with us?"

"Taking what?"

"The story."

"Where?"

"With us. Going forward."

"Are we going forward?" From his bed, Cze smiled at her.

"Yes."

"How would we tell the story?"

"I don't know. Maybe a fiction?" Anya adjusted her bed to the seated position.

"Collaboratively?"

"Yes." Anya gazed out the window from her hospital bed. "I'm glad I got the bed by the window," she said turning to Cze. "Would you like me to tell you what I see?"

"Is there something?" He tried but could see only sky from where he was.

"Moving truck. They're bringing a piano into the hospital." She used the lever to raise the bed — to get a better view. "I miss him," she said watching the movers roll the piano across the sidewalk. "It takes three movers to move a piano," she said as they moved the piano into the hospital through the automatic doors. Then she shifted gaze to the sky. The cloud patterns in the sky. Her heart hurt. "We should have worn helmets," she said softly. Then she watched the sky until sleep.

Cze slowly got out of bed. Grabbed his cell phone. He sat on the edge of the bed again. Dizzy. He could hear the nurses chatting down the hall. Once he got his bearings, he padded out the room and into the visiting area. Quietly, slowly he dragged a chair to the west-facing window. Managing seemed a modest success. He took the Lego piece from the hospital gown pocket. Placed it on the sill. He fidgeted with it, tipping it on its right side, then left side, bottom, and top. He stared at the Rocky Mountain range clear in the distance as he made the call.

"Hello?" It was quiet. Cze knew it was his son. He held the Lego piece tight. "Deck?"

Nothing but breathing.

"Decker, I know you're there. I have one question for you."

"Hm?"

"You interested in seeing the mountains one day?"

Cze sat with the silence for a long time. He had forever to wait. He carefully touched his shaved head. Thirty-two stitches itched.

"How will I get there?" the boy asked.

"You'll fly. Okay?"

"Okay."

More breathing.

"Dad?"

"Yes."

"You know she died? You know Mom died, right?"

There was so much silence.

"She didn't vanish. She's dead."

Those words coming from his son cut through him. "Yes. I remember."

"How come it took you so long to know?"

"I don't know."

"Okay."

Cze began to weep ever so quietly.

"Dad?"

"Yeah, bud."

"It's okay."

On August 7, 1934, he dissected the word **agrarian**
studied the awkward rhythm of it
gazed at the serifed geomancy for some time
the descending **g** *unstable he suspected*

On August 7, 1939, in his fifty-first year, he examined the
word **arid**
this triangle of tarpaulined land required considerable
irrigation,
there was that spilling sun and that ascending dead-end **d**
he was struck by mindless grief when the crops failed again
and again

At one hundred thirty years old he had been considering the
word **home** *for quite some time*
having navigated the storm clouds to the east china sea
through the **o**
and possessed with a corvine urge for **umi budo**
he dove into **nirai kanai.***

---

* The gods reside in the underwater realm known as *nirai kanai.*

REDUX

August 1, 2044 —

SLOW.

So slow, she receded.

At this point in life, uneventful was fine. Kate MacNeale had even come to terms with agonizing over loss, grief, and solitude. In Paris she could actually imagine the slow beauty in that kind of ideology. In fact, there were *lycées* that delivered such secondary curricula peripheral to their religious studies program. Quietude was an academic discipline. As part of the post-pandemic movement, many companies had diversified and dedicated themselves to the hidden-existence culture, to serving the life of the mind. Along with her laptop and the old-fashioned books (as her son referred to them) she'd brought several virtual and traditional streaming services such as SpotifyAH playlists that included holographics and the aromatization of rain, ocean, and florals. Most importantly, she had brought Zhen.

Zhen was Kate's cat. Since the beginnings of the global pandemic over twenty years ago, cats had become popular companions for the new breed of agoraphobic. At this time, more than any other in history, it was widely observed that having a cat as a companion contributed significantly to healing, wellness, and mental health. It was as simple as that. The status of the cat and its ubiquitous acceptance rose in even boutique hotel establishments such as Leica. *The place.* She simply wanted to burrow in obscurity amid a curation of silences — here at this place, in Room 362, where she was convinced Nick's essence lingered.

The virus. There were so many sudden deaths beginning in 2020. In some cases, and for whatever reason, the spirits seemed to stay. Stayed in places, in spaces and landscapes, and even within the living. Not an assumption that she alone possessed. There had been thousands of documented sightings, miracles, and phenomena surrounding the people who had suddenly died. Though these *ghosts* were ephemeral, there were means to regenerate.

How to Restore a Loved One in Two Ways:
1) HoloG
2) Self-manifestation

If the new technology was available in their locale and if they could afford it, some had their loved ones reanimated through the HoloG procedure. The arrangement was as costly as a mortgage on a house. It was one of those big-ticket items that couldn't possibly be considered if massive layoffs loomed or work was precarious. One kept in mind, therefore, that for many the decision was unfortunately fettered by employment instability and the generational post-pandemic fallout. But if one could — and was tolerant of version glitches — HoloG was certainly a way to bring back a loved one. The downside was that the capacity to touch and hold was limited, and once you had arranged for the HoloG procedure, self-manifestation — the second means of bringing back a loved one — was impossible. Yet self-manifestation was the ideal method of revival. Though uncommon, despite the time commitment — and the related risk of sinking into madness — it was more desirable than HoloG. For rather than mere facsimile, self-manifestation produced a full-fledged resurrection. Only about a hundred cases of self-manifestation had been documented since 2020. But it was possible. The process began with finding *the place*.

Leica was their place.

An unplanned stopover in Paris.

Between Cambridge and Ezra.

They attended the international summer program at Cambridge in 2019. He was so bright that scholarships and study tours came easy, as did bursaries in those early years. Nick seemed to land everything he sought. In his heart, a seed small and powerful: he couldn't squander opportunity for it was everything that his interned grandfather never had. Kate had a theory that Nick was the genius and she, a mediocre student, simply rode on his study-travel coattails. The truth was that they complemented and prodded each other. She saw pale things: how soft midday shadows fell and travelled over the walls and desks during Jacobson's Block D international development lectures; how classmate Zhao Li described with detailed brilliance the AI chess assignment he was doing back home in China and then how timid (in a lovely way) he became when asked in Literature III class to deliver an oral analysis of Spenser's *The Faerie Queene;* and while ear-budded, Kate recognized how the water fountain in the confines of the Asian and Middle Eastern Studies Library vestibule complemented the music of her Sawako playlist. That was the magic of their relationship. They saw the world differently in some ways, the same in others.

While at Cambridge Nick focussed on Asian studies and took a series of workshops and seminars offered by Ryukyuan scholar Dr. Setsuko Oshiro. There was also research he wanted to conduct in the many libraries. Kate was more interdisciplinary and chose to take in the afternoon neuroscience, churchyard architecture photography, and artificial intelligence plenaries at Selwyn. She found that the discourse from English-fluent learners from across the Asian continent took inclusive student engagement to a level she was not accustomed to. In this classroom she thrived on the diverse dialectic rigour of forward-thinking global voices outside of the Western theoretical sphere.

But it wasn't the study that Kate remembered most about the sleepless summer school stretch. It was the pre-class and late-night excursions with Nick. She would ache throughout the lecture-filled days for those drifts of passionate randomness in the romantic dawns and nightfalls of Cambridge corners. Her most beloved memories were of those early mornings when the sun, despite following on the heels of retiring shadows that knew, failed to expose their alcove embraces; and in the evenings in dusky passageways so well hidden that even the ancient starry nights were oblivious.

As planned, after the semester at Cambridge was complete, they took the train to Paris. But before heading to Roissy and taking the non-stop Air Canada Arrow back to the prairies, they lingered for a few rainy days.

On the first evening in Paris they stumbled into a dark nook from which jutted a sullen wooden sign hanging on a wrought-iron arm. Carved into the sign: *LEICA of the Obscure Ways, established 1821.* Soaked, shivering, bedraggled, they huddled within beneath what could only be described as a broken-hearted portico. They knocked tentatively at the door, almost not wanting it to open. But it did open — to sanctuary.

Pilgrimage. Every year since Nick's death, when she could once again travel, Kate had escaped to the refuge of the Parisian hotel to immerse herself in books and writings. Her doctoral focus was influenced by the preliminary research that Nick had conducted on the Ryukyuan Archipelago. Though not a typical student, Kate had intention. She had stretched her studies with the hope of engaging in collaborative work with her son, Mak. While Kate studied as a PhD student, her son completed his course requisites and was now a candidate focussing on the tail end of his field work and dissertation. Here at Leica for these two weeks, it was time for power reading in preparation for her own upcoming comprehensive exam. The refuge had developed into a summertime tradition that served to inspire Kate's academics, restore her soul, and bring her back to *the place*.

"Coffee, madame?"

"Yes, please. Does it still come with warm cream?"

"Of course."

"Thank you."

"Would you like a copy of the *New York Times* this morning?"

"Do you have the traditional print version?"

"We do," he said from beneath the mask.

"Print, then, please."

"Very good."

"Thank you. The rotary phone and retro colour scheme in my room is very thoughtful." She tried to imagine what he might look like behind the mask.

"I'm glad you like them. There are also large umbrellas on our rooftop patio. Flowers. Particularly beautiful this year. Warm rain. Good surroundings for your studies."

"I'm fine here. You remembered?" At that moment Zhen brushed against her ankles. She noticed remarkable white hair askew.

"I remembered," he said. He picked up a tablecloth that had fallen.

"Perhaps tomorrow. That would be luminous." Luminous? She felt somewhat embarrassed. At that moment she recognized the distinction between words written and spoken, intentionality, consequence. She proceeded to the front page of the newspaper: "#SkinWars: Twitter Presidencies of the Past."

Kate MacNeale   August 1, 2044 at 11:36 PM
To: Nick Holt
Re: and again

Dear Nick,

It was raining when I arrived. Pouring small then big. And that freakish moment you and I enjoyed that first time we visited Paris. Remember? Once again it thrilled me: the taxi driver circled randomly (or with chaotic expertise?) around the Arc de Triomphe amid a cyclonic scribble of cars and buses, exited the spirographic symphony onto a street corner where looking over my shoulder I happened to glimpse the extended foot of the Eiffel Tower. No matter how many times I have seen it over the years, the tower's foot planted amid the congested city core fills me with wonder and terror.

Are you here?

Kate

August 3, 2044 —

KATE HAD ALWAYS ENJOYED hiding in things that possessed creative/creation potential — a pencil that leaned toward B, a Greek tragedy, a blank piece of paper that didn't bleed, a scalable four-letter word in vector format, a prepped and loaded camera, Nick's shadow, instrumentals. The latter this morning in the form of Peder Bjørnstad's weather-appropriate brooding compositions. Still and yet and here and why Kate embraced the simplicity and nothings of circular field-recording meditations hidden in Paris days.

She watched as Zhen moved quietly, predatorily around the bottom of the sheers as they wavered and bloomed in the breeze. After *ess*-ing around the undulating white cloths, the creature leapt with a graceful arc onto the bedding — old *noro* priestess's kimono with its cotton layers, soft and worn. Waiting for the brew, Kate watched Zhen curl, groom, close her sapphiric eyes, stretch long, and settle into *shavasana*.

August 5, 2044 —

THE DAYS CONTINUED TO BE. To be so quotidian-quiet that Kate was under the delusion her trip would continue in this manner. As she'd planned and hoped.

She leaned on the balcony with coffee in hand. The rain fell onto the cobblestones, travelled down crevices and runnels, between interstices and increments, and puddled. Rain bounced off the plastic webbings of black umbrellas and mingled with scant light, muting the bright florals on *façades* and balconies.

Searching for the vanishing point down rue Copernic Kate discovered there wasn't one. She leaned against the wet railing and looked up at the expanse of grey. All thoughts of work, deadlines, worries, and pain taken in this moment by each raindrop that washed her.

After a long, hot bath, Kate planned her day with less-is-better in mind. Towel-drying her hair, she wandered to the dresser where three cameras were rowed. She popped open the hinge mechanism of the rather amusing and cumbersome black box. Inserted the film. Closed it. The film cover ejected. Carried on with rubbing her hair. This was Nick's vintage camera, which he had used as a struggling artist — when he was a furniture illustrator. The challenge: one must be discriminating about the use of the film, as one shot was basically all the photographer had. This was completely unlike the more forgiving digital Canon and the old 35mm Fuji. Just then Kate caught sight of pale flickerings. From behind the bed, the cat stared unblinkingly at her with a contagious fear, as though she knew she was beginning to fade — greytoning and desaturating. Kate was familiar with the signs.

Kate MacNeale August 5, 2044 at 10:58 PM
To: Nick Holt
Re: . . .

Dear Nick,

How much rain can the sky hold?

That is to say, nothing from here has infinite capacity does it?

Our time together was incomplete. Though there are certain things I cherish and will always miss. That is why I have been relentless in trying to evoke you.

However, this is the last trip to Paris for me.

Last small words . . .

I love you.

Kate

August 13, 2044 —

"GET THE FUCK OUT OF THE WAY!" he yelled as he ran toward her.

She froze.

Black rain cape, wild. Countless black umbrellas fell away on cue as if he'd parted the mouth of the Champs-Élysées. He knocked her to the ground. Kate instinctively cradled the camera as her head hit the pavement. Her mind raced.

Before she knew, he'd hooked her neck with his left arm and with his right hoisted a gun on his hip. He quickly pivoted in the direction of the military eight-pack advancing from the 8th arrondissement to the east, and then swung to the southwest where another three sets hedged, all taking a knee and gun-ready. Helicopters with harnessed soldiers leaned out from doors flung open and angled down to Kate and Black Cape. Others circled above searching for Black Cape's collaborators. The sounds of big boots sucking up the wet street in a synchronized slosh. Then guns cocked and loaded on cue. The instant of global lawlessness over. Policing had become unforgiving.

It happened instantaneously. She struggled to get out of Black Cape's grip.

He constricted her neck, her face toward his. From beneath the plastic hood that tented his face: "Stay put. I'll break your neck. I'll do it, bitch."

No identifiable accent. No mask. But his eyes and lowered brow, his skin, his mouth. For a split second he was lucid: he softened and in the pale of his eyes she saw the fear of a lost boy — a young man, about the age of her own son, Mak. She wondered what his story was and how he had gotten here. Was it through the Skin Wars, desecration activism, crushed by the countless economic depressions, mental and physical breakdown, a victim of circumstance, or a combination of all of the above?

And it rained.

On him. On her.

Large drops crushed the city. Like holy water for the masses it came down on Paris.

But unrelenting rain...

"Help," he managed with despair. In a blink his eyes were filled with some sort of origin-humanity. Soul recaptured in between seeking a million small mercies and sifting through knowing final confessions. She shuddered for they both understood, here and now, he had fallen to a point of no return. Rivulets of rain streamed off his black plastic hood and over his eyes, his face. This lost boy with the pale eyes. Then he switched back to distant and retightened his grip around her neck.

She was snagged upward with a forceful jerk. She was certain this was all a dream. But these days it was difficult to know. As she looked down from above, Black Cape appeared sacrificial, surrounded by the shrinking perimeter of soldiers. His body twitched with each assault before falling still into a small black heap. Theatre. All ground players diminished as she rose, then vanished completely.

In flight, Kate noticed from the corner of her eye, through the slate sheets of rain, that the Arc de Triomphe holographic projection had been taken down, exposing the monument's partial ruins, the result of the initial post-pandemic Skin Wars attack over twenty years ago. The outline of the monument indistinguishable. At that moment she wondered how much of the city landscape and the rest of the world had been cosmetically altered. Did anyone really know the measure of what was real, how much of their world was imagined? She soared through the air. Over the Eiffel Tower, its holographic façade had also been dismantled to reveal its broken bones. With the perceived terrorist threat on the Arc de Triomphe, National Guard security had been dispatched to protect all cultural landmarks. The sound of concentrated gunfire cut through the sheets of rain.

Literally unscathed, she was very gently let down in front of the Leica portico. Had she mentioned the hotel? No. Do helicopters taxi victims about like this? Amid the cacophony, there was no one delivering her. There was no helicopter above that she could see or hear and no one at her side. The rain fell so hard that sightlines were blunted by monochromatics. The hidden military, they too the colour of rain, hustled past her in phalanx formation. Sirens blared, from somewhere something hissed, and a stream of police cars blurred by. The camera dangled from her neck as she ran into Leica. She glimpsed a figure at her heels. But when she took a closer look there was no one following but the rain.

She laid the camera on the dresser — there in the space between the Canon and the Fuji.

Stared in the full-length mirror.

"Zhen?" she asked in a soft voice. She unwrapped the wet garland of a scarf that twisted around her neck. She fumbled with the buttons on her coat. In the mirror, watched her fingers shake with each unbuttoning. Her eyes glistened like amber as tears streamed down her cheeks. Zhen jumped up on the wooden console near the mirror. The tiny mews were enough to soothe. Kate removed all her wet clothes. They lay in a heap of muddy grey. She studied her naked body. Moved her neck slowly, then her limbs. No broken bones and no sign of blood. She made her way to the bed, curled up in a fetal position, pulled a blanket around herself, and cried. Zhen circled near and settled into a small comma.

Kate MacNeale August 14, 2044 at 5:58 AM
To: Sam Makishi Holt
Re: son

Son.

That's all.

I just wanted to see the word there on (air quote) paper.

Love, Mom

Sam Makishi Holt　　　　　　　August 14, 2044 at 11:58 PM
To: Kate MacNeale
Re: hey

Mom,

You okay?

Either you are in the depths of writing — it must be poetry —
or you're having a breakdown.

This collaborative research you and I have embarked upon
seems heavy on my end at the moment. As you can imagine.
So get your shit together over there, okay Mom? Haha.

I will need help when we get back together in Ezra.

Dr. Miyashiro has arranged for the University of the Ryukyus
to put up for the cost of a boat to get us a little closer to the
Diaoyu/Senkaku and the other Ryukyu Islands that have risen.

Now that the Ryukyus are independent, I wonder if the
Diaoyu/Senkaku will officially belong to them. Well, the risings.
Dad would be shocked that this is the outcome of his prelim-
inary work. I'll be conducting a string of interviews. Yes, yes,
I'll adhere to our previously outlined oral history methodology.
Can you send me the ethics consent form? Thanks, Mom.

One last thing: be mindful of Zhen's lifespan. You can't let her
drain dry. Impossible to charge then. Maybe deactivate.

Mak

August 14, 2044 —

KATE WAS TAKEN by how, in practice, Mak seemed so like his father at times. The academic-subversive style in which he wrote papers; the near obsession with field work photos, sketches, and other multi-modals; and how he not only annotated but painstakingly hieroglyphicized etymologies in the margins of textbooks and articles. Kate wondered if the scholarly idiosyncrasies Mak possessed were organic to his nature and to what degree influenced by what he knew of Nick through artifacts. It had also crossed her mind that the last two decades of trying to manifest Nick may have cross-wired in transference somehow.

Kate was weary with thought.

Madness. Loneliness. Sadness.

It would not be unreasonable, even for the casual observer, to recognize that she was falling.

The phone rang. Startled.

"Oh? Really? I don't remember ever —"

Pause.

"However, as you say that would be perfect right about now. Thank you."

She didn't know how he knew.

Promptly at eight o'clock there was a knock at the door. She found a tray with a complimentary bottle of rosé, a slice of pepperoni pizza, two small chocolate truffles, and a holograph bouquet of white daisies and chrysanthemums. At ten o'clock she found her journal and a black marker and proceeded to sketch out a comparison chart of Nick and Mak. By the darkest hour the flowers had faded and she'd emptied the bottle.

August 16, 2044 —

THE MORNING SUNLIGHT filled the rooftop patio. Peace. There was little to reveal that there had been rain-soaked days or an incident of terrorism. She fleetingly wondered, as the sound of silence was so loud, to what degree violence had been normalized.

Only a bit of the wine hangover lingered. Kate set the box of research material down beside her chair and gently laid her laptop on the glass-topped table. She found her SpotifyAH, then set the floral hologram playlist to circle at the lowest speed, scaled at 430 degrees, diagonally looped at forty-five degrees, fluctuated between three and eight percent opacity with Kosemura playing almost imperceptibly in the background. She leaned into the cushion of the patio chair and prepared for a day of reading — "Suiteki" first, and then to a place "where women carry piglets on their heads and people walk barefoot."*

* Shun Medoruma won Japan's Akutagawa Prize for his short story "Suiteki." The quotation comes from Baku Yamanokuchi's renowned dialogic poem *Kaiwa*.

A light breeze caught her dress — layers of diaphanous pale grey fluttered up and wrapped her legs.

"Good morning, madame."

"Good morning."

"Will you have coffee?"

"Yes, please."

"Would you like a newspaper?"

"Thank you."

"You're welcome." There was a pause. "May I ask if there is anything at all that we can do for you?"

"I'm just going to read for the day. Thank you."

"Yes, of course." And then, "May I ask you something?"

"Yes."

"Are you okay?"

"Yes."

"You must have been quite frightened."

"Yes. I was frightened." At that moment she wished more than anything that she could be held.

"I'm sorry it happened."

"Thank you."

"Of course."

"The rosé last night —"

"I hope you enjoyed it."

"Yes, I did. Thank you."

"You're welcome."

"Wine is a weakness of mine."

"Yes."

"It's a shameful thing to have to admit."

"Well, I wouldn't say so; wine is quite divine. So why not be divined?"

Though conversation was muffled due to masking, for the first time she heard the timbre of his voice. Kate tried to look into his eyes. "I —" The sun silhouetted him. After all these years of annual stays, he remained the constant.

"Would you like a light brunch in time?"

"Does it still come with the crepes?"

"Yes."

"Does it still come with a fresh boiled egg on toast?"

"Yes."

"Yes, please."

"Of course."

"Thank you." In trying to see his face, she held her arm over her eyes to shield from the sun.

"These umbrellas are not properly protecting you from the rain forecast for this afternoon. I'll have them moved to suit you as you read throughout the day. I'm sorry for all the rain."

"I was hoping for rain, though. There is little rain where I am from."

"I have always thought that reading while the rain falls can be a pleasurable experience."

"Yes. The sound of rain."

"Yes. The sound of rain."

Kate MacNeale
To: Sam Makishi Holt
Re: the rise

Hi Mak,

No worries. I'm not falling apart — yet.

But honey, there was a terrorist attack near the hotel the other day. Did you hear about it? How much have these kind of incidents become normalized? I wonder if we have all become desensitized over time. Well, let's talk about it when we're back in Ezra.

Xia Steph et al. said that the East China Sea Plate shifted in 2022 followed by the slow geographical rise of islands of the Ryukyu Archipelago. Do you have the exact parameters on the rate of the rising and the current distance the shoreline floats on the rock pillars above the East China Sea? Are you getting those analytics from the existing scholarship? Straight from the horses' mouths? (You won't know that one; it's an ancient saying.)

It must be an incredible sight. The islands floating above the East China Sea.

Love, Mom

August 17, 2044 —

AFTER THE DAYS of considerable distraction (to say the least), Kate made some progress with her comprehensive exam readings. She had fallen into a good routine on the Leica rooftop. On this day she planned to read some related diaries, memoirs, and journals. This type of archive had proven invaluable in understanding frontline Ryukyuanist praxis.

A few books on the table had toppled. One, a notebook of Nick's, had slipped out of its loosely tied cinch and fanned open. Kate could see the inked handwriting, the pencilled marginalia of key words, text-wrapped cartographies, and small sketches of multi-disciplinary notions. She recognized some as the ones he'd emailed her early in 2020. It was the journal he had composed while in China studying the Diaoyu/Senkaku Islands. At that time his focus was less on Taiwan's claims and more on the China/Japan dispute that heightened in 2019 after the Okinawan prefectural city of Ishigaki made a municipal name change to the disputed islands and called them Tonoshiro Senkaku. Assertion in the waters from China escalated. Japan forged allegiance with other countries experiencing similar micro-aggressions and they began to report China's activities to one another. This, combined with so many issues, including America's postwar military presence in Japan — which focussed primarily on the largest of the Ryukyuan islands, Okinawa — and the tug of war for the Diaoyu/Senkaku and its natural resources, erupted in a clash of the titans. Nick had no way of knowing the outcome of the Ryukyuan Islands. He couldn't have imagined the otherworldly island-by-island rise of the kingdom that once upon a time paid tribute to China, and after the Satsuma conquest and Japan's annexation gradually became the nation's most impoverished prefecture. Tangentially, Kate wondered if some of the related scribblings and other elements in the notebook could be converted into holographic visual elements for use in a SpotifyAH playlist. There was little to be gained straying as she did with these types of concerns. She refocussed.

Sam Makishi Holt
To: Kate MacNeale
Re: distance

August 19, 2044 at 10:02 PM

Mom,

The keynote speakers presented yesterday. It's mostly natural scientists but some interdisciplinary lectures over the next couple days, too.

I did a few sketches from the field trip out to the islands, and then incorporated lecture analytics with Photoshop. There's flexibility if we create our visual series this way (multi-modal research portfolio) — maybe blend the raster and vector-based graphics when necessary. Statistics were interesting. The distance between the Ryukyu Islands and the East China Sea is 1.487 kilometres. Not quite one mile. Hopefully later on they'll address the rise rate over the last couple of decades.

The rise between the Ryukyu Islands and the East China Sea is 1.487 kms

↑
↓

EAST CHINA SEA

A few more lectures and the roundtables are scheduled for today. I'm looking forward to geophysicist Rai Nakashima's presentation of her recent paper on the physical phenomenon of the rise. There is a breakaway dialectic on the post-rise relationship between China, Japan, Korea, and the U.S. Let me know if you'd like to join via Zoom. I'll register you for online access. Overall, a great conference.

Oh, and I noticed Ito lurking about — seeding and tweeting incendiaries.

Looks like you're up early tomorrow. Direct flight out of Roissy.

No doubt you've got a couple weeks' worth of the New York Times in your luggage.

Have a good trip back to Ezra!

See you there.

Mak

August 21, 2044 —

Kate woke bleary-eyed and foggy-headed. Disoriented, her whereabouts not immediately apparent. The room was small: door to the right, the window to the left, a ceiling fan above, and rather than the sounds of rain outside she could hear wind gusts. Oh, yes. It was her own bedroom in Ezra and not Leica in Paris. The pocket watch on the nightstand read four twenty a.m. She conducted a half-hearted inventory: body scan, mental scan, life scan. It didn't take long to realize — or rather to remember — how sad she was. Though why she was sad was not exactly clear, and she had neither the energy nor the desire to self-diagnose.

Zhen, now reactivated, lay asleep at the foot of Kate's bed. The sight of the cat eased her. But the creature was once again beginning to pixelate and break up. She was counting on her son to restore Zhen once he returned from the conference. Mak had said the technology had improved in recent years and it might be worthwhile to consider an upgrade. Over time, Kate had developed loyalty to things that worked (processes, relationships, routines,

267

technology versions), and HoloG no exception. As far as Kate was concerned, they would never be able to reproduce the perfection of this iteration of Zhen. Once again, she was thinking too much, and each thought was becoming entangled with unrelated thoughts. The pills she had taken the night before seemed to re-anesthetize her. She fell back into sleep.

In her early-morning second sleep Kate experienced a serial-format nightmare with installments that provided little intermission for escape. Her sleep was fitful.

Finally, at nine fifty a.m., she awoke rather exhausted. She had slept longer than intended. The autumn sun was so bright that it lit up the bedroom despite the horizontal blinds and shone through the knife-line gaps shadowing the wall. Normally, the morning sunshine in and of itself would make for a good start, but today the relentless Ezra wind along with the nightmares and jet lag resulted in a migraine.

She reached for the pocket watch on the nightstand. It had belonged to Nick's grandfather. The only personal item of value that survived the internment camp days. It was Nick's cherished possession — it resided on the nightstand being useful. Other than judging light on the horizontal blinds, it was the only means of telling time in this bedroom. She held it in her hand and put it to her ear as its quiet mechanics and the feel of its worn silver casing in the palm of her hand soothed. After a few minutes she placed the pocket watch back on the nightstand.

She needed water. On the way to the bathroom Kate tripped over stacked luggage and then slipped on clothes that were strewn in clots down the hallway. Once in the bathroom she went through the morning ritual. Fumbled squeezing the toothpaste onto the toothbrush and it was precisely at this moment she could hear rustling about the house. She became still. Nothing. She wondered if Mak had come home from the Ryukyus. It would be a week early, if he had. Or perhaps Zhen had gotten into something. Kate quieted the running water as the mysterious sounds persisted. She tried to identify what the sounds were and from where in the house they emanated. Quiet. All seemed quiet. She continued to brush her teeth, then wash her face.

Her pulse quickened. Coffee? There was the aroma of coffee in the air.

She was gripped with both inquiry and fear.

"Mak?" She slowly walked into the kitchen expecting to see her son. A copy of the *New York Times* lay folded on the kitchen table. Pages of sketches and a couple pencil stubs. A man was at the window, pouring coffee, his back to her.

She moved toward the door. Prepared for flight.

He turned.

Kate was filled first with confusion, then with terror.

At a distance she searched his face, but that brilliant Ezra sun was at his back darkening his features. She semicircled. Contours remained unknown until at last, the sun fell upon his face.

"It's — it's you. How?"

"Yes. Don't cry."

"Where were you?" she asked, searching his face.

"Nearby."

"Why'd you leave?"

"I'm sorry." He slowly, gently wiped her tears.

"It is truly you?"

"Yes."

"I was waiting for you."

"I know."

"Why did you take so long?"

"I tried. Every manifestation is different. There were moments."

"Were there?"

"Faintly. Mostly when you were afraid. And when you wanted warm cream with your coffee."

"Yes. As I recall, there was something."

"Was there?"

"Yes, something."

"Something," he whispered.

She kissed him.

"I was always there — in Zhen, the rain, reflections, music, Leica, even in the eyes of the pale boy —"

"Nicholas. Just hold me slow."

And he did.

He held her slow.

Inspired by Art Tamayose
1934–2021

ACKNOWLEDGEMENTS

Many thanks to NeWest Press general manager Matt Bowes for his belief in the first story written for this collection, "The Ryukyuan." His patience in waiting for each story over a stretch of time meant a lot to me. I am grateful to my editor, Leslie Vermeer, for her guidance, expertise, and kindness; and to the behind-the-scenes efforts of Claire Kelly and Natalie Olsen.

I wish to acknowledge my family (two at the heart, many in between, and Art and Naoko at the helm); my extraordinary friends; and my post-secondary community of supervisors, colleagues, and classmates.

DARCY TAMAYOSE is a writer, graphic designer, and PhD student. Her work, which includes the novel *Odori* and youth fiction book *Katie Be Quiet,* has received the Canada-Japan Literary Award and has been shortlisted for both the Writers' Guild of Alberta's Georges Bugnet Award and the Foreword Indie Juvenile Award. Born and raised in the prairie landscape of southern Alberta, Tamayose lives there today surrounded by daughter, family, and friends.

SHORT STORY COLLECTIONS AVAILABLE
FROM NEWEST PRESS

¶ This book is typeset in Domaine by Klim Type Foundry, with sans serif details in Freight by Joshua Darden.